BARBARY WHARF

Harlequin Presents and bestselling author Charlotte Lamb welcome you to the world of Barbary Wharf.

In this fascinating saga, you'll experience all the intrigue and glamour of the international world of journalism. You'll watch the inner workings of a newsroom, share the secrets discussed behind closed doors, travel to the most thrilling cities in the world. Join the players in this high-stakes game as they gamble for the biggest prize of all—true love.

In *Besieged,* you'll meet Nick Caspian and Gina Tyrrell, whose dramatic story of passion and heartache unfolds throughout this series. And next month the saga continues with another sizzling romance between characters whose careers—and hearts—intertwine in the most captivating way.

Don't miss these unforgettable romantic adventures each month in Harlequin Presents—the most popular romance fiction series in the world.

The Editors

CHARLOTTE LAMB is one of Harlequin's best-loved and bestselling authors. Her extraordinary career, in which she has written more than one hundred books, has helped shape the face of romance fiction around the world.

Born in the East End of London, Charlotte spent her early childhood moving from relative to relative, to escape the bombings of World War II. After working as a secretary in the BBC's European department she married a political reporter who wrote for *The Times*. Charlotte recalls that it was at his suggestion that she began to write "because it was one job I could do without having to leave our five children." Charlotte and her family now live in a beautiful home on the Isle of Man. It is the perfect setting for an author who creates characters and stories that delight romance readers everywhere.

Books by Charlotte Lamb

A VIOLATION
SECRETS

HARLEQUIN PRESENTS
1370—DARK PURSUIT
1393—SPELLBINDING
1410—DARK MUSIC
1435—THE THREAT OF LOVE
1467—HEART ON FIRE
1480—SHOTGUN WEDDING

Charlotte Lamb

Besieged

BARBARY WHARF

Harlequin Books

TORONTO • NEW YORK • LONDON
AMSTERDAM • PARIS • SYDNEY • HAMBURG
STOCKHOLM • ATHENS • TOKYO • MILAN
MADRID • WARSAW • BUDAPEST • AUCKLAND

Harlequin Presents first edition October 1992
ISBN 0-373-11498-2

Original hardcover edition published in 1992
by Mills & Boon Limited

BESIEGED

BARBARY WHARF

CAST OF CHARACTERS

Sir George Tyrrell—The elderly owner of the *Sentinel,* one of Britain's most prestigious newspapers.

Gina Tyrrell—The young widow of Sir George's beloved grandson, James, she is personal assistant to Sir George at the *Sentinel.* Devastated by her husband's death, she devotes herself entirely to Sir George's well-being.

Nick Caspian—International media tycoon with playboy reputation. Owns and operates newspapers all over Europe, and has now set his sights on Britain—starting with the *Sentinel.*

Piet van Leyden—Chief architect for Nick Caspian's newspaper group, eager to take over supervision of the Barbary Wharf complex. Blond, Dutch and charming, he travels extensively around the world and is fluent in several languages.

Hazel Forbes—Gina's loyal colleague at the *Sentinel* and secretary to Sir George. Efficient and businesslike, she appears to have no time for outside interests—including love.

Roz Amery—Foreign affairs correspondent. The daughter of an international journalist, she is fiercely ambitious.

Daniel Bruneille—Chief foreign affairs editor. Rules the department with an iron fist. Fiery and temperamental, he is nevertheless admired and respected.

PROLOGUE

For more than one hundred years, London's Fleet Street has been the heartbeat of Britain's major newpaper and magazine industries. But decaying buildings and the high cost of inner-city real estate have forced many companies to relocate dockside, down by the Thames River.

The owner of one such company, Sir George Tyrrell, has a dream, a vision of leading his newspaper, the *Sentinel,* into the twenty-first century with a huge, ultramodern complex called Barbary Wharf. But money and time are running out for Sir George, and he fears that his dream—and perhaps even the newspaper—will die.

Enter Nick Caspian, international media tycoon. The man with all the money, desire and the means to take over the *Sentinel.* Will he succeed and if he does, will he change the *Sentinel* beyond recognition? Will he change the life of Gina Tyrrell, a woman who understands his desires? And what of the people whose lives are entwined with their loyalty to Sir George and his paper?

CHAPTER ONE

IT WAS a raw winter day, Barbary Wharf swirled with river mist, and Gina was worried about the old man. Her slanting green eyes watched him all the time: the way he was leaning on his walking-stick, his slow gait, the stoop of his shoulders. He was too old to wander around a draughty building site on a day like this, but every Monday morning before he drove to Fleet Street he insisted on stopping off here to talk to his architect, to plumbers, electricians and builders, side-stepping piles of bricks, or even rubble which hadn't been cleared away yet, dodging under ladders and scaffolding.

He got irritated if she said anything, of course; he hated to admit he was no longer young. She found it hard to believe, herself. He had seemed amazingly young to her when she'd first met him, only eight years ago— Sir George Tyrrell, nearly seventy then, but a giant of a man, broad-shouldered, upright, with an energy younger men envied. Today, he was a shell of the man he had once been, and it had happened overnight. From the day his grandson died, the old man had turned grey and weary, the spring of his life broken.

She sighed, her long russet hair blowing back over her shoulders as a gust of wind from the river hit her. Five years. Was it really that long since James had died? It seemed like yesterday, although when she looked into a mirror she could see how time had changed her, too. She had been twenty the day James died; she felt positively

7

middle-aged today. Sometimes she wished her own life had ended that day, too.

A darkness entered her green eyes. Sometimes she almost thought it had ended.

'You're shivering, Gina,' Sir George said, joining her. 'Why didn't you wait in the car, like a sensible girl? You shouldn't be standing around in this weather!'

'Nor should you,' she said, smiling at him, and he gave her a wry smile back.

'Now don't you start nagging again!'

'Nagging? Me? As if I would!' Gina said, and he grinned.

'Well, don't. I'm fine, quite capable of visiting Barbary Wharf for an hour without collapsing! It's you young ones who don't have the stamina——' He suddenly broke off, stiffened, staring at the entry to the site. 'What the devil is he doing here?'

His angry voice made Gina jump. Looking round, she saw three men walking towards them. She knew one of them: an expensively dressed, slim-built man with pale brown hair and a rather too ready smile. She had never liked him very much—he was too polite to be genuine— but he was a partner in the merchant bank which handled Sir George's affairs, and the old man had always seemed friendly enough with him. Why should he object to Mark Huxley visiting Barbary Wharf?

'Has Mark done something to annoy you, Grandfather?' she asked tentatively.

'Mark?' Sir George said slowly. 'Oh...yes, Mark's with him. I hadn't noticed him before. Now, what the devil does that mean?' His brows worked furiously. 'My God, what is Mark up to, bringing him here, behind my back?'

'Him?' repeated Gina, puzzled. So he had not been referring to Mark? 'Who. . .?'

'Nick Caspian,' Sir George muttered, and Gina's green eyes widened. She knew that name, although she had never met the man or even seen him before.

'Isn't he——?' she began, and the old man interrupted.

'He's an octopus, that's what he is! He owns newspapers in most European countries, except this one—and his tentacles stretch further every year. He'll be global before the end of the century.'

'That sounds positively frightening!' Gina said lightly, wondering why Sir George was so upset.

He didn't smile. 'Believe me, it is! He wants to start up over here now, and he's after the *Sentinel*.'

Gina took a deep breath, her eyes widening. 'But...but he couldn't possibly get control!' Then she gave him an uncertain look. 'Could he? I mean, you still own a majority of company shares, don't you?'

Before Sir George could answer the three newcomers joined them. 'Good morning, Sir George, Gina,' Mark Huxley said smoothly. He was smiling, but the old man turned unfriendly eyes on him.

'What are you doing here?'

Mark's smile did not falter, nor did he try to answer the question. Instead, he said, 'I think you've met Mr Caspian, Sir George? And his associate, Piet van Leyden?'

'I've met them,' growled Sir George, scowling.

'But I don't think you have, Gina?' Mark enquired, rhetorically, since he obviously knew the answer to his question. 'This is Nicholas Caspian—Nick, Gina Tyrrell.' He did not explain her relationship to Sir George, which made her suspect that he had already done so.

The taller of the two men held out his hand. She automatically put out her own and felt it swallowed by firm, possessive fingers. Her green eyes lifted in a startled gaze. She could see why the old man had called him an octopus. She had the uneasy feeling that she might never get her fingers back.

'Mrs Tyrrell!' he acknowledged in a deep voice, his hard grey eyes narrowed in their inspection of her face.

She almost stammered as she replied. 'How do you do, Mr Caspian?' He was a shock, at close quarters: an electric dynamo of a man, pulsating with an energy she felt crackling up her hand and into her body, making her nerves leap and her blood run much too fast.

He wasn't handsome, but she knew she would never forget that face: chiselled and hard-boned, it mirrored the strength and grace of his body. He had the streamlined power of a black panther, and yet he reminded her of the old man in some odd way which puzzled her.

They didn't look alike, but there was something in the eyes, in the set of the jawline, that was oddly reminiscent of Sir George. His fashion sense was rather better, though. Sir George wore classic suits which he had bought years ago and intended to wear until they fell to pieces. Nick Caspian wore stylish clothes: a chic dark grey suit, made by an excellent tailor; a white silk shirt in the latest style; a wine-red silk tie. His clothes had class, and so had he.

How old was he? Thirty-five? Thirty-seven? Had he inherited his newspaper empire? She couldn't help feeling curious about him—all she knew about him was gossip she had read in the popular Press, which was ironic, since he made his money selling such newspapers.

'You work for Sir George, I gather?' he asked, his brows lifting in a faintly mocking amusement. 'As his personal assistant?'

She nodded uncertainly, because the title sounded far too important for the work she actually did.

'So you know all his secrets,' drawled Nick Caspian, and she felt Sir George bristling beside them.

'I don't know any secrets!' she quickly said, before Sir George could explode again. Her voice was low and husky, because while she was staring at Nick Caspian he had been returning the compliment, and his assessment of her features had been thorough and disturbing. He took his time to study her face with its finely moulded cheekbones and jawline, the warm pink mouth, softly curved and full, the almond-shaped eyes, misty with startled uneasiness, the straight, silky hair which was the colour of leaves in the autumn. Gina found his stare so unnerving that she wanted to pull her hand out of his grip and run away, but that was out of the question. She had to stand her ground and pretend to be very cool.

She was relieved, though, when he let go of her, and she could turn hurriedly to greet the other man Mark was introducing.

'Piet van Leyden, Gina.'

Piet van Leyden was much younger than Nicholas Caspian; he was thin, in his early thirties, not much taller than herself, with smooth blond hair, bright blue eyes, and very brown, well-weathered skin which made her wonder if he worked out of doors, or merely spent a lot of time in some sunny part of the world. He was more casually dressed, in amber-yellow cord trousers, a tweed jacket and a yellow sweater over a white shirt.

'How do you do?' she said, and he smilingly answered her, lifting her hand to his lips to kiss it with a graceful gesture.

'A very great pleasure,' he said softly and she flushed, very self-conscious while Nick Caspian was watching them.

'Do you work in the newspaper business too, Mr van Leyden?' she asked huskily.

'In a way. I must tell you how impressed I am by the architecture of this complex, Mrs Tyrrell. I have not seen anything so striking in Britain before.'

'Oh, do you think so?' she doubtfully murmured, looking around them. Barbary Wharf's unusual red and black brick walls, the black glass windows which looked like mirrors, the octagonal structure, were ultra-modern. They had been specially designed to house a state-of-the-art printing works in the basement, and above that floors of air-conditioned, ultra-modern newspaper offices, where everything possible was computerised and standardised. It had been hailed as avant-garde, but Gina wasn't sure she liked it. She found its modernism aggressive.

'You do not?' Piet asked, looking amused. 'Oh, but look at that banding, the Greek key patterning in the brickwork! And the shape, the octagon! The glass lifts and elevators! The open-plan floor space which can be split up easily with movable screens. So many features of the complex are new and exciting, I think.'

'And damned expensive to build!' Sir George grunted, still scowling.

'You don't get quality at a bargain price!' Piet said with a trace of scorn.

'Piet is an architect,' Nick Caspian softly dropped into the conversation. 'And a damned good one!'

'Thank you,' Piet said, giving him a sideways grin then looked at Sir George directly. 'As an architect, of course I have an ulterior motive for believing that a good architect is worth whatever you pay him, but, believe me, I do admire your architect, and you, Sir George! It was brave of you to choose such a forward-looking design, and I envy your architect this riverside site. He has used the setting well. I am very impressed. I wish I had been involved in designing this complex.' He caught Nick Caspian's sardonic gaze and flushed a little. 'But I work exclusively for Caspian International, so I couldn't have put in a design for the competition you held,' he quickly added.

'You speak very good English,' Sir George grunted. 'Do you work here all the time?'

'No, I work all over Europe, wherever Caspian International needs me to supervise a site,' the Dutchman said.

Out of the corner of her eye, Gina studied Nick Caspian. He had no trace of an accent when he spoke English, although he certainly looked foreign. Was he a Latin, she wondered? Mediterranean, perhaps? He had that colouring—the black hair and olive skin.

'You still haven't told me what you're doing here, Huxley!' Sir George demanded abruptly.

Mark Huxley coloured, glancing at Nick Caspian with uncertainty, and it was Caspian who answered, his deep voice curt.

'I asked him to show me round.'

Sir George ignored him, speaking to the banker. 'Not very polite, is it, Mark? Taking this fellow round my new complex without asking me first?'

Mark Huxley was deeply embarrassed, his face darkly flushed. 'I'm sorry if I have inadvertently offended you, Sir George, but Mr Caspian is one of the bank's most important clients...'

'And I'm not?' the old man growled, chin jutting belligerently.

Mark Huxley made unhappy noises, and Nick Caspian shrugged. 'If it's going to cause trouble, we had better leave, Mark.' Before moving, however, he raked back a strand of thick black hair which the wind had blown across his face, considering the old man with an odd mix of grimness and what to Gina looked surprisingly like compassion.

'But listen to me, Sir George,' he said quietly. 'You can't refuse to face facts for ever. Sooner or later, you are going to have to talk to me.'

.'Get out!' raged the old man, the blue veins in his temples bulging so much that Gina paled with anxiety.

'Please...you're upsetting him...please, just go,' she broke out, putting her arm around the old man, and appalled to discover that he was trembling.

'Don't beg, Gina!' Sir George growled, pushing her away.

Nick Caspian's cold eyes met hers briefly, and he frowned. 'There's a phone in my car outside. Shall I ring for a doctor?'

Sir George made a convulsive move, breathing thickly. 'Will you get out or must I have you thrown off the site?'

'He's an old man, and this could be too much for him!' Gina protested, her small face stiff and white and her green eyes shadowed.

Nick Caspian gave an abrupt nod, and without another word turned and walked away, with the other two men hurrying after him.

'Let's go, Grandfather,' Gina whispered, sliding her arm around him again. It was bad for him to get so angry, but how could she stop him flying into one of his rages? He had always had a furious temper, and he was too old to change, and, anyway, she was too fond of him to want him to be anything but himself. But she was afraid that one day he would lose his temper once too often, and die of it.

'Don't treat me like a child, Gina!' he grunted, but leaned on her heavily, let her carry the bulk of his weight until the chauffeur saw them coming and leapt to her assistance, helping his employer into the back of the sleek limousine.

He leaned back there, breathing thickly, as the car moved slowly away. They were on their way back to Fleet Street, but Gina anxiously wondered if she could persuade the old man to go home, for once.

She opened her mouth to try, when he suddenly burst out shakily, 'I sometimes think I'm under a curse. I've lost everyone who ever mattered to me . . . my wife first, dying of cancer while she was still a young woman, and then our son, Jack, killed with his wife in that plane crash.'

He swallowed, audibly, and she held his gnarled hand, gently stroking the dry, cracked skin, the crooked fingers which had been stiffened by arthritis into these rigid shapes. He so rarely talked about the past, or about anything personal. He avoided anything which could be called emotional; he was not a man who liked letting anyone guess at his feelings. For him to talk like this something must be very wrong.

'You shouldn't brood over the past,' she said quietly, but he wasn't listening. He was talking as much to himself as her. His eyes were bloodshot, his skin as yellow as wax, and she was worried by the way he looked.

'I wished I had died with them, but there was their son. James was only seven when they were killed; he needed me.'

'He loved you dearly,' Gina said gently, and he smiled at her then, his eyes regretful, though.

'But I worked harder than ever, to help me forget, and that meant I didn't see much of James. I left him with other people all the time, and I felt guilty about not spending enough time with him, so I spoilt him, I suppose. Gave him presents, let him have his own way, have whatever he wanted...'

Including me, she thought bleakly. James had met her when they were both seventeen and still at school. At eighteen, he had asked her to marry him. They had been ridiculously young, and they had loved each other with the wild intensity of innocence. James had been desperate to marry her. She would have waited. Gina had a deeply rooted common sense which had urged her to think twice about such an early marriage. She had adored James, worshipped the ground he walked on, but she had felt too young to start on the responsibilities and problems of married life.

Her father had been alive then, and he had been horrified. He had protested, tried to refuse consent, and she had half hoped he would, although she loved James so much she couldn't refuse him anything. But James had won, because he could twist everyone around his little finger, including his grandfather. Sir George had ridden roughshod over her poor father, who was a shy, nervous man. Sir George had made his viewpoint crystal-clear. If James wanted her, James must have her, and so she and her father had given way.

To be fair to him, he had been as kind and indulgent to her from that moment onwards, as he was to James. She had become his grandson's wife, and that made her one of his family—and when her own father died, not long before James had his accident, Sir George had been so thoughtful and gentle with her that she had learnt to love him very much. Under his gruff exterior she had found he hid a tender heart, especially where the young were concerned.

'And then I lost James, too, in that stupid accident— reckless young fool!' Sir George grated.

She felt tears well up in her eyes and turned her head away, running the back of her hand across her eyes.

'I'm sorry, my dear,' the old man groaned. 'Clumsy of me, clumsy and tactless. I know it upsets you to talk about him...'

'But it's true,' she said sadly, 'James was wild and reckless.' Hadn't that been partly what had attracted her in the first place? She had been young enough to be excited by his wildness.

'Yes,' the old man said grimly. 'It's true, and it was all my fault. I spoilt him. He was too used to getting his own way. If I had taught him to use his brains, he would never have tried to jump that fence on a horse that he couldn't control. And he would be alive today.'

'You shouldn't blame yourself!' Gina said huskily, her face white between the long, smooth strands of her russet hair.

'You have a kind heart, my dear,' he said grimly. 'But the truth is, I always put my business first and my family second.'

She knew some people who would agree with him—he had plenty of critics, if not outright enemies—but she couldn't see the point of blaming him at his age for the way he had lived his life, or for being the man fate, or nature, had made him!

'If I lose the *Sentinel* now, it will be a judgement on me,' he said, suddenly, and she turned her head to stare at him in shock.

'Lose the *Sentinel*? What are you talking about?'

He sighed, his head bent, his gaze fixed on the floor. 'I suppose you have to know sooner or later.'

'Know what?'

'We've got problems, my dear.'

'Problems? What sort of problems?'

'Money,' he bitterly muttered. 'Finance. We have cash-flow problems. What the City calls a "serious financial difficulty", and the man in the street calls "going broke".'

She was stunned, staring at his averted face. He had never breathed a word about any of this to her—but that didn't surprise her. Although she worked in his office he still kept her very much in the dark as to what he was doing. She knew most people thought he had created the job just to give her something to do after her husband died, and there was some truth in that, she couldn't deny it.

She had had a secretarial training, but she had been only twenty when she became a widow, and she was only capable of doing a very junior job. Sir George would not hear of that, though. He said it would embarrass him to have his grandson's widow working at such a low level. Nor would he let her work for some other company—that would be equally embarrassing for him, he said. He pleaded with her to let him take care of her, to keep her near him. He said she was his last link with his dead grandson, and he would miss her if she left his house, his firm. Gina had been helpless to argue any more after that. It comforted her own grief to know that she was needed.

At first, there had been nothing much for her to do. She had had to invent her job herself, gradually realising that there was a vacuum in the large and busy office surrounding Sir George. He had plenty of secretaries who could type and use word processors, file, answer phones. What he needed was someone who would always be on hand to look after him personally; make his life easier; keep people away from him, including his senior secretary, on occasions; act as buffer between him and the world; talk to people he did not want to offend but did not want to talk to himself; act as his eyes and ears in the company; play go-between when members of the staff had a grievance they could not put forward through 'usual channels'. Gina became, in a sense, an extension of Sir George himself, but only in certain areas. She knew little about the financial details of the company.

Sir George's chief secretary, an acid middle-aged woman, had resented Gina's arrival on the scene, and had given in her notice, perhaps in the hope of forcing Sir George to choose between them. It had been a mistake; Sir George had accepted her resignation with a courtesy which barely disguised his relief at getting rid of her, and had immediately promoted one of the more experienced younger women, Hazel Forbes, to take her place.

Hazel was just a couple of years older than Gina, but she was a calm and clear-headed girl. She had no problem taking over the running of the large office, she found it easy to keep the rest of the staff in order, and in a short while she and Gina had become friends, once Hazel was sure that Gina would not try to undermine her, or get her job.

Their friendship was not a close one, however. Gina was too shy. Since her husband's death five years ago, she had not even had so much as a date with another man. She had had tentative approaches from men now and then, but she had always politely frozen them off. She had loved James fiercely, and been too badly hurt when he was killed to want to risk falling in love again.

She knew far more about Hazel, who was very pretty, and popular with the opposite sex, although so far she had never seemed really serious about any of the men she dated.

Hazel was discreet when she mentioned her work, however. If she was aware of the problems besetting the firm, she had never breathed a word to Gina, although, like everyone else who worked for the newspaper group, Gina had known for a long time that the firm was having trouble with this move from Fleet Street down to the riverside, some half a mile away. The first stage of the new complex should have been finished months ago.

By now, in fact, they should have moved down to Barbary Wharf from the old nineteenth-century building in Fleet Street from which the *Sentinel* newspaper had been published for eighty years. Instead a succession of strikes and accidents, delays and disputes, had held up work at every stage, and so, far from having moved out of the Fleet Street premises, they had not yet even sold the building.

'Has it cost too much to build Barbary Wharf?' she asked Sir George, who shrugged.

'That's part of it. The original estimate was for two hundred million . . .'

She gasped. 'How much?'

He smiled wryly. 'Yes, it sounds like toy money, doesn't it? I wish it were. We borrowed it through Warburton and Grenaby—in the beginning the interest rates were half what they are now. If the building had not taken so long we might have been able to repay the loan before the interest rates began to rise. As it is, the interest keeps going up, and we are barely paying off the interest, let alone the loan itself.'

Gina's pale brows met as she grappled with the problem. 'Won't it help when you sell the old *Sentinel* building?'

'Obviously it would,' Sir George said irritably, 'if we could! But so far we haven't found a buyer. The London property market is in a very bad way. And that isn't the end of our problems. Because of this recession, advertising revenue has taken a catastrophic dive. Suddenly our income has dropped, our costs have gone up—and we still have to pay back this loan.' He gave her a quick, frowning look. 'Now, not a word to anyone about this! There's a board meeting this week, and God knows what will come out of that.'

She knew them all, the well-fed, well-dressed, blandly smiling men on the board of directors. They would have to find somebody to blame if the worst happened, and their scapegoat would undoubtedly be Sir George Tyrrell. The Barbary Wharf project had been his from the beginning.

It had once been a wharf from which ships sailed to the Barbary coast of North Africa, to bring back ivory, oranges, spices, carpets, beaten copper and silver ware— and for Gina the very name was exotic, romantic. She remembered visiting the tall, gloomy warehouses, their windows grey with cobwebs, their cavernous depths empty at last. They had stood along the riverbank for over a hundred years. She had not dared venture far inside, but had stood near the tall double gates, peering in and seeing the air dusted with gold as sunlight fell across the walls. She had almost been sure she could smell oranges, but that must have been her imagination. The warehouses had gone now, bulldozed down in a few hours. They were only a memory. All that remained was the name.

Sir George had been planning this shift out of Fleet Street for a long time. He had bought Barbary Wharf for the company at what was a knockdown price, a few months after she and James were married, but it had taken years to get planning permission. Powerful lobbies had fought tooth and nail to stop the project for one reason or another, but eventually Sir George had won, and work had begun: the warehouses were bulldozed down, the site cleared and the foundations laid. The walls had slowly begun to rise towards the sky. By then, though, James had been dead, and some of the fire and power had gone out of the old man.

The limousine pulled up outside the *Sentinel*'s old offices in Fleet Street, and the chauffeur came round to open their door and help Sir George and then Gina out.

She gave the chauffeur a smile. 'You go and have a cup of tea, John. You must be cold. We'll ring when Sir George wants you to take him to lunch. He'll be eating at his club today.'

She slid her hand through the old man's arm, feeling him lean on her more than usual. Every day, he seemed wearier. They made a slow progress across the pavement, through the swing doors, into the lobby which had the dim, high ceiling and tiled floor of a Victorian railway station. Inside they could hear the rumble of machinery far below in the basement printing works, the sound of phones ringing, the echo of voices in the shabby offices on the ground floor.

The doorman saluted and hurried to hold back a lift; the receptionist murmured a polite greeting. Sir George nodded, said good morning to one of the editorial staff, smiled at a secretary on her way up to her own floor. He liked to feel that he was keeping in touch with the people who worked for the *Sentinel*, although, since James died, he no longer took a slow stroll around the newspaper every day, as he once had.

'Cold morning!' he said to everyone else in the lift. There was a chorus of agreement, as he expected, but nobody tried to engage him in conversation. Gina frowned slightly, looking at their polite faces. He had become a remote figure—did he realise that?

The chairman's offices were on the top floor. As they got out of the lift, Gina said, 'I wish you had told me how worried you were! It might have helped to talk about it. You carry too many burdens.'

'I didn't want to load my problems on to your young shoulders! In fact, the last thing I wanted to do was talk about what was going on. I was trying to keep it very hush-hush, and when I began to get approaches from Caspian it was disturbing. I wondered where he got his information from! Now it's obvious!' The old man's eyes blazed. 'The bank has sold us out.'

Gina gave him a troubled look. 'What do you mean?'

'They're our chief creditors. If they think we might not be able to meet our debts, they may have made a secret deal with Caspian.'

'Surely they wouldn't do that? Isn't it unethical for a bank to make such a deal?'

Sir George laughed grimly. 'I doubt if ethics trouble them.'

They had reached his office; he stopped to stare at the gold plate on his highly polished mahogany door. 'CHAIRMAN: Sir George Tyrrell', it read.

He gave a bleak little smile. 'I've spent the last few years planning this move to Barbary Wharf. Be ironic if I leave the *Sentinel* before we even leave this building, won't it?'

She leaned her cheek against his arm in a tender gesture. 'You'll think of something! Don't be defeatist. There must be a way out!'

He kissed the top of her silky head. 'If there is, I'll find it!' he promised.

In his office, she helped him take off his thick cashmere overcoat and hung it in the en-suite cloakroom leading out of the office. Just as Sir George sat down behind his desk, Hazel appeared; crisply neat and slender in a dove-grey pleated skirt and blue shirt, her dark brown hair softly bobbed around her oval face.

'Just in time for your first appointment!' she said, laying a folder in front of him. 'I've made the coffee— shall I pour you a cup now or wait until Mr Dearden arrives?'

'I'd like one now,' Sir George decided, opening the folder and slipping on his reading glasses. 'Bring a cup for Dearden, too, though.'

'Do you want me to stay while you see the editor?' asked Gina, because he sometimes asked her to sit in on his morning conference with the editor of the *Sentinel*.

'Not this time, my dear,' he said, already beginning to read.

She followed Hazel out, and, as the door closed behind her, said, 'I really need a strong coffee! I'm freezing, after standing around Barbary Wharf for so long, and he looked frozen too. I wish he wouldn't insist on going there so often.'

'Tell him, he might listen to you!'

'I'm hoarse with telling him, but he takes no notice!'

Hazel did not look surprised. She knew the old man almost as well as Gina did, by now. She was a first-class secretary; cool and immaculately dressed, anticipating every want of her boss, able to read his mind at times— she was really too good to be true!

Gina gave her a wry smile, collected her coffee and went through to her own office. She had a mound of paperwork in her in-tray. Many departments tried to reach Sir George through her these days, in the hope of by-passing Hazel, who defended her boss against un- wanted intrusion. They were always disappointed, since the last thing Gina wanted to do was upset Hazel, but Gina glanced at the memos and letters, all the same, in case they held something important, and then she went through her copy of Sir George's schedule for the day. As he had no evening appointment she rang their home, and spoke to the housekeeper, Mrs Thomas, to suggest a dinner menu, with a wine she knew Sir George enjoyed. Gina drank very little wine, but Sir George liked to have a good wine on the table.

As she hung up, she knocked a pile of today's newspapers off the edge of the desk and bent to pick them up. One of them fell open; a photograph stared up at her. With a start she recognised Nick Caspian, in evening dress, his arm around a stunningly lovely blonde whom she recognised, too, as Christa Nordstrom, a Swedish model who kept turning up on magazine covers lately. Was she Nick Caspian's latest girlfriend?

Gina refolded the paper and put it back on the pile. She had too much work to do to waste time speculating on Nick Caspian's private life. She began to make phone calls—one of them to the foreign news room to talk to an old school-friend, Roz Amery, who had only recently got a job on the paper.

'How are you liking life on the *Sentinel*, Roz?' she asked, smiling.

'It has its moments!' Roz said guardedly, in her deep, smoky voice, and Gina frowned.

'Something wrong?'

'Can't talk now,' said Roz. 'How about lunch soon?'

'Today?'

'Great. What time?'

'Twelve-thirty? Do you want to go out, or eat here, in the canteen?'

'Out, if that's OK with you.'

'Sure. I know, let's be tourists—I'll see if I can book a table at the Cheshire Cheese, shall I?'

Roz laughed. 'Why not? Or we can pop into some other local pub—and eat a salad sandwich. See you down in the lobby at half-past twelve.'

Typical of Roz not to waste time! Gina thought wryly. Even at school she had known what she meant to do. When they were ten years old, Roz had proclaimed that she was going to be the best foreign correspondent in the world one day. She had gone to university to do a language degree, and then single-mindedly headed for Paris to work for a year on a news agency specialising in sending French news to London newspapers. From Paris Roz had gone on to Rome for a few months, and then Berlin, before managing to land a scholarship which sent her on a year's tour of the world. She had sent back stories from every place she stopped *en route*, and when she got back Sir George had given her a job on the *Sentinel*.

Gina often envied Roz her clear vision of what she wanted from life. Gina was nothing like so certain. In fact, she seemed to have drifted from moment to moment, place to place, like a jellyfish. She always seemed to have allowed other people to make her decisions for her—first James, then his grandfather.

When she rang the Cheshire Cheese, a world-famous Fleet Street pub which was on the tourist map and usually crammed to the door with Americans and Japanese, to her surprise she managed to get a table for two, a last-minute cancellation, she was told.

She had only eaten there once, years ago, but remembered their steak, kidney and oyster pie with respect. She must recommend it to Roz.

There was a brisk knock on her door and still smiling, she said, 'Come in!' The door opened and she glanced across the room, her eyes opening wide as she recognised Nick Caspian.

'You!'

'Me!' he agreed, closing the door and strolling towards her. The mocking amusement in his face made her suddenly angry.

'What do you want?' she snapped at him. 'You can't see Sir George. You upset him enough this morning, appearing at Barbary Wharf out of the blue, like vultures swooping down for a kill! I don't know which of you is the worst—you or the people at the bank! Anyway, I'm not going to let you see him again today.'

He sat down in a chair on the other side of the desk without answering, his head tilted to one side, his long, lean body calmly in repose, one leg crossed over another, a polished black shoe swinging.

The grey eyes were unreadable, enigmatic. In fact, his face had no expression on it at all—even that air of amused mockery had vanished—but she hated his cool self-assurance.

She felt a fool; she had lost her temper and she hadn't so much as made a dent in his armour. Deeply flushed, she said miserably, 'Oh, why don't you go away, and leave him alone?'

'I didn't come to see him,' Nick Caspian said softly. 'I came to ask you to have dinner with me.'

CHAPTER TWO

GINA couldn't believe her ears. 'What did you say?'

He twirled his shoe, contemplating the sheen on the toe-cap. 'Do you like Greek food? I've heard very good things about a new Greek restaurant that has opened in Mayfair. Knighton Street—isn't that close to the Tyrrell house?'

'You've got the nerve of the devil!' Gina was so angry her voice almost shook. 'You're trying to ruin someone I love very much, yet you walk in here, cool as a cucumber, and ask me to have dinner with you!'

'If you love Sir George——' he began, and she interrupted.

'If you're trying to get to Sir George through me, you can forget it! He wouldn't ask my advice about business matters. I have no influence with him whatever.'

'Keeps you in the dark, does he?' drawled Nick Caspian.

She gave him a cold stare across the desk. 'I am not going to discuss Sir George or his affairs with you.'

Her icy front did not seem to dismay him. He considered her with thoughtful grey eyes and asked, 'How long is it since your husband died?'

She got even angrier. 'And I'm not discussing my private life with you, either!'

'Any men in your "private" life?' he drawled, and her skin burned.

'Get out of my office!'

'I didn't think there were!' His eyes glinted with amusement, and she was so furious that she almost shouted at him.

'I didn't say that!'

She only realised how unwise the angry denial had been when she saw the mockery in his smile.

'You didn't have to say it—it's obvious.'

Her slanting green eyes fell and she frowned. What did he mean by that? Why was it obvious that there was no man in her life? She glanced at the mirror on a wall opposite, wishing she were alone and could stand in front of the mirror studying her face for traces of whatever Nick Caspian had seen.

'As I was saying, if you really care what happens to Sir George you will have dinner with me, so that we can talk about this situation!' he said, his relaxed pose infuriating her because she herself could not relax; she was as tense as a stretched piece of elastic. It made her nerves vibrate just to be in the same room as him.

'I'm busy,' she said shortly.

'Another date?' he asked and she hesitated, not liking to lie, then nodded.

He stared, eyes hard and narrowed, then was on his feet a second later in a movement so smooth that she didn't realise what was happening until she saw him standing on the other side of the desk. She blinked, startled, and then he was on her side of the desk. It was like a conjuring trick—now you saw him here, then he was there, but how he got from one place to the other was a mystery.

Gina felt her nerves jump. She shrank back in her chair, looking up in alarm as he loomed over her.

'W...what d...do you think you're doing?'

He sat down on the edge of her desk, leaned over and took hold of both arms of her chair, spun it round so that she faced him, his mocking grey eyes inches from her own.

She was wearing an amber wool dress made from a Liberty print based on a William Morris art nouveau design. High-necked, with long sleeves, and a smoothly fitting waist and long, flowing skirt which reached mid-calf, it was faintly medieval. It covered most of her body while emphasising the very feminine curve of her figure, and Nick Caspian deliberately let his eyes wander down over her from her straight russet hair to what he could glimpse of her slim legs and small, elegantly shod feet. It was a very personal stare, and she resented it, her skin flushing pink.

'I don't believe you have another date!'

'I don't care what you think!'

'Then why lie to me?'

Her chin came up and she gave him a defiant look. 'All right, I won't! I don't have another date, but I have no intention of having dinner with you.'

'That's better,' he said coolly. 'I prefer straight talking, even when it is an insult.' He watched her lashes flutter down against her flushed cheeks, and even with lowered lids she could feel the way he was staring. After a moment, he said, 'Sir George is acting like a fool, but you don't have to copy him, however fond of him you are. If you're sensible, you'll talk to me. Climb down from your high horse and agree to have dinner with me.'

Her green eyes flashed. 'I don't know if that is a threat, or blackmail, but whatever it is, it won't work. I'd rather jump out of that window than have dinner with you.'

He laughed out loud. 'Excuse me if I beg leave to doubt that! Leaping out of a twelfth-storey window seems a rather desperate way of refusing a dinner invitation.'

She felt silly again, and knew he had intended she should. She was beginning to recognise his technique. His cool grey eyes taunted her silently, and she decided she did not just dislike him, she hated the man. Gina had always thought of herself as quiet and low-key, certainly not the type to make wild threats or want to hit a man with something heavy, but Nick Caspian was having a very odd effect on her metabolism. She had never had such explosive thoughts, and that disturbed her even more. Ever since she was eighteen and had married James she had been reminding herself that she had to be adult and mature, she must never forget that she had become a Tyrrell and wherever she went people would be watching her. It had not been easy, in the beginning, but she had trained herself to be cool and in control, even when James was killed and grief ate her up—and she was not losing a grip on herself now, however much Nick Caspian annoyed her.

She took a long, deep breath and tried to sound remote, but firm. 'Look, do I have to ring Security and ask them to remove you from my office?'

The threat left him unmoved. Worse, it made him even more amused. 'Is that supposed to frighten me?' he asked, staring at her mouth, and she felt her lips tremble, as if he had actually touched them. Appalled, she instinctively put a hand up to hide that from him, and he laughed again, softly.

She was beginning to think he had powers that seemed almost supernatural; or how else did he manage to read her mind so easily?

'Was there ever any man except your husband?' he asked in a voice that sounded casually curious.

'Get out!' Gina hissed, her hands screwing into small, pale fists.

He looked down at them, his brows lifting in quizzical comment. 'Now why do I get the feeling you want to hit me?'

'Because I do!' she burst out before she could stop herself.

He laughed. 'You're full of fascinating contradictions. On the surface very demure and sweet, but there's a positive volcano bubbling away under that, isn't there?'

Gina was so startled that she was dumb, and that made him laugh again.

'Well, much as I'm enjoying our little chat, I'm afraid I have an early lunch appointment so I'll have to go soon——'

'Good!' she snapped.

He gave her a wry look. 'Sir George has got to be made to see reason! I gather he's as attached to you as you are to him—so, despite your claim that he won't ask your advice, I'm sure he'll listen to you. You must make him understand that he has no options left. Whether he talks to me or not, I am going to take over the *Sentinel*.'

'He'll find a way out,' she said with stubborn loyalty, and Nick Caspian contemplated her with an odd expression, his grey eyes level and almost gentle.

'I almost wish, for your sake, you were right!'

She felt a little shiver run down her back. At that instant, she began to be really afraid for the old man. There was a cool certainty about Nick Caspian that frightened her—he had the look of a man who knew he would win, who was unstoppable. But she lifted her chin and stared him out.

'I know him; you don't!'

'I know a damn sight more about his present predicament. It's a classic business trap—an old-established firm decides to make radical changes, expand, build new premises, borrows a lot of money and gets heavily into debt.'

It was precisely the picture Sir George had drawn for her earlier, in the taxi, and she was horrified to realise how much Nick Caspian knew.

'I told you, I'm not discussing this with you!' she said fiercely, and tried to get out of her chair, but he caught hold of her arms, leaning even closer.

She tensed, her ears drumming with awareness. 'Let go of me!'

'Not until you've started listening properly! You don't know much about the business world, I'm afraid. Sir George has no hope of raising any more money, except by selling either the new complex, which would make a nonsense of his whole strategy for the past ten years——'

'He'll sell this building, not Barbary Wharf!' she impulsively said, and he gave her a dry glance.

'It has been on the market for a couple of years without selling!'

She bit her lip. He knew too much. How could the bank have betrayed the old man's confidence like this? Or was it just Mark Huxley who had conspired with Nick Caspian? Did the other partners at the bank know what had been going on?

'There have been offers,' she protested, knowing that none of those offers had been acceptable. A few people had tried to get the building cheaply, but Sir George was not yet that desperate. 'Any day now,' she said, 'it will be sold and then they can repay a large part of the debt.'

'And in the meantime, how are they going to pay the monthly instalments on the repayment?' Nick Caspian drawled. 'At present, as you must know full well, the company is having difficulty just paying the monthly wages bill.'

Her green eyes opened wide in shock. The old man had said nothing about that to her. Of course, she did not have anything to do with the accounting side of the business, and he carefully excluded her from financial and board meetings. But surely she would have heard some rumours? This place was a positive hive of gossip about everything from the latest love-affair to the current state of salary negotiations the management were having with the National Union of Journalists. If the problems had been that serious she would have heard whispers from the accounts department.

Nick Caspian watched her, his mouth crooked. 'I'm afraid it is true, Mrs Tyrrell,' he shrewdly informed her, having read her expression with disturbing accuracy. 'They're living from week to week, barely keeping ahead of the bills which come in. Their cash flow has been badly hit. Their ability to keep up their repayments depends upon having a larger income entering their bank account—and they don't have it.'

'How do you know so much about the company's private affairs?' she furiously accused.

'I have my sources,' he coolly told her. 'Believe me, I know what I am talking about. The income is slipping all the time. They are just not making enough money. They can only get out of trouble by finding a fresh injection of capital.'

She stared at him, her face pale.

'Which is why the bank have been talking to me, and why I have been trying to talk to Sir George. I might invest in the company, on certain conditions.'

'The bank had no right to talk to you!'

'They have every right to protect their investment. They have shareholders, too, you know, who expect to get a profit on the money they invest through the bank, and certainly expect to get their money back. I'm one; I have a holding in the bank. That is why they talked to me.'

'They shouldn't have told you anything about the private business of another customer!'

'They didn't have to tell me what was happening—I already knew,' he said curtly.

'Well, you would say that, wouldn't you?' she scornfully threw at him. 'I expect the bank want you to keep this little conspiracy a secret.'

His hands tightened their hold on her arms as if he would like to shake her. 'There is no conspiracy! Do you really believe that any company could get into this sort of deep water without other people finding out? I've heard gossip about Sir George's problems all over Europe. I was told about it in Berlin. I heard whispers in Paris. Europe is a small world. These days you can't keep anything quiet for long.'

She bit her lip, forced to believe him. She had seen straws in the wind herself; she had known for ages that there were problems, although she had not realised how serious they were.

Huskily, she said, 'Well, anyway... it wasn't ethical for the bank to plot with you...'

'They didn't,' he insisted. 'I went to them to ask how much truth there was in what I had been told. I was looking for a newspaper group in England to invest in, and I thought that, if it was true that the *Sentinel* was in trouble, I could make a deal with the proprietor.'

'Even so, they had no right to talk to you behind Sir George's back!'

'They didn't,' he insisted. 'They tried to talk to him on my behalf, get him to see me and discuss a possible deal—but he refused to consider the idea.'

'Are you surprised? You want to take his company away from him!'

He raked a hand through his thick, black hair, frowning. 'At his age he should have retired, anyway. He's far too old to cope with all the stress and anxiety of such a huge company, especially during a time of trouble—look how he's coping with the problems at the moment. He's behaving like an ostrich, pretending that there is no danger when it gets closer every day. It's obvious what the company needs—more capital, a pretty hefty investment from somewhere. Yet when I offer just that, Sir George refuses to talk to me! Can't you see that is plain crazy?'

'I don't know enough about it to pass judgement,' she said slowly, but she was impressed by what he had just said. The company needed new investment, obviously—but Sir George must have good reason for refusing to talk to Nick Caspian. He was frightened of him, frightened of his motives and secret aims.

'Oh, yes, you do,' he said, moving even closer, and she pressed back into her chair to get away. He had in-

vaded her body space and she was so disturbed by that
that she could actually hear the blood surging in her ears.
This close to him, she could see the graining of his skin,
the black glitter of his pupils, the harsh angularity of
his cheekbones. She had told herself he wasn't good-
looking, but he had an intense masculinity which was
making her breathless. She couldn't take her eyes off
him.

'If the company goes bankrupt it will leave chaos for
whoever has to pick up the pieces,' he was saying, and
she watched his mouth moving, hypnotised. His lower
lip had a passionate curve that riveted her attention—it
could look hard, determined, but it had a sexual promise
that made it hard to look away.

'Sir George wouldn't let that happen!' she whispered.

He bit out curtly, 'How will he stop it?' Then, with
wry emphasis, he added, 'What about all those jobs that
are being threatened? What about all the other firms
who supply the company? The creditors who could all
lose their money? Once a company has gone bankrupt
it's very hard to put it back on a healthy footing.'

She found herself believing him, convinced by what
he had told her, by the direct, dominating stare of those
grey eyes.

Slowly, she said, 'Barbary Wharf alone is worth
millions...'

'Yes, the company still has very valuable assets, but
once confidence in a firm has gone people will start
selling shares and the price will fall like a stone. It's
falling now. Not fast yet, but remorselessly.'

Gina looked at him sharply. 'I would have thought
that would favour you! You must be able to pick up
shares cheaply.'

'I am, of course,' he admitted, smiling wryly. 'Nothing significant as yet, because large blocks of the shares are held by people who aren't selling or can't sell—like young Slade, whose father's estate hasn't been legally proved yet. I need enough shares to give me a seat on the board, so that I'm able to influence the way the company is run.'

He sounded so reasonable. Why was Sir George so much against him? 'It's a pity you visited Barbary Wharf without asking his permission first,' she said. 'He didn't like it. It has made him suspect you.'

He grimaced. 'I realise that. If I'd known he was likely to be there, I wouldn't have gone, but I had only seen it from a distance, and I wanted to take a closer look before I made a definite commitment to buy into the company. It is a fascinating piece of architecture, and I would have enjoyed looking over the complex even if I hadn't been thinking of investing in the company. Piet was dying to go round it, too, while he was over here in London for a few days.'

Her eyes lit up. 'He was very taken with it, wasn't he?'

'He was very taken with you, too,' Nick Caspian said with a sardonic smile.

Gina was startled into silence, blushing to her hairline.

'Don't look so surprised,' Nick Caspian drawled. 'I thought he was pretty obvious about it, myself, and I'm sure you knew you had made a big impression. He couldn't take his eyes off you, but I'd better warn you— Piet is a charmer, but no woman ever holds his attention for very long, so I shouldn't get involved with him.'

'I have no intention of getting involved, as you put it, with either of you!' she said, pink and off balance.

'But you will have dinner with me tonight? I can see you don't know enough about what is going on—and if you are to help Sir George, I think you should be better informed.'

That made sense. If she was to help the old man, she had to know more about his problems. Slowly, she nodded. 'But only on the understanding that I am on Sir George's side, and I'm not doing anything that could hurt him.'

'You have made that crystal-clear!' he said. 'Then I'll pick you up at——'

'No,' she interrupted. 'He mustn't know I'm seeing you, or he will be furious.' It was an understatement. In his present mood, Sir George was seeing conspiracies everywhere, and she didn't want him to doubt her loyalty. 'I'll meet you at the restaurant. I know the one you mean, although I've never been there. The Knossos. It's just around the corner from where we live. I can walk there in two minutes.'

He nodded. 'OK. Eight o'clock?'

'I'll be there,' she said, and had hardly finished speaking before he was walking across the office. She looked, blinking, at the door as it opened. He moved like lightning. He frightened her.

'See you,' he said softly, and made it sound alarming. The door closed, the office was silent, but Gina couldn't move. She sat behind her desk staring at nothing, remembering the strange intimacy of talking to him, the mockery of his smile, the authority he conveyed when he chose, and the air of menace he could conjure up. She had never met anyone like him.

There was a rat-tat-tat on the door and she started. 'Come in!'

Hazel appeared, round-eyed and curious. 'Who was he?' she breathed. 'He was here for ages! Was it OK to let him in without warning you?'

'I wish you hadn't,' Gina said grimly. 'I'd like a four-minute warning next time. He can be a shock to the system.'

Hazel grinned. 'I bet! I'm sorry. When I said I would buzz you and tell you he was here, he wouldn't let me. He said he wanted to surprise you!'

'He certainly did that!'

'Well, tell me all about him,' Hazel insisted. 'Who is he? How long has it been going on? And why didn't you tell me about him?'

'You've got the wrong impression,' Gina began, 'He isn't...' Then she broke off, realising that if she told Hazel who he was she would have to swear her to secrecy or she might blurt out something to Sir George, and that would not be fair to Hazel. It would place her in a false position. Better not to tell her anything.

Her long silence had intrigued Hazel even more, unfortunately. 'What isn't he?' she probed, grinning. 'Serious? Don't you think he's a long-term prospect? Well, he's so sexy, that wouldn't surprise me. He must have a woman in every port. But who says love has to be long-term or serious? Make hay while the sun shines, that's my motto. I should grab him while he's interested, if I were you.'

'I'm not that desperate for a man!' Gina said, flushed and furious.

'I know that!' Hazel quickly said. 'That wasn't what I meant... but if you fancy him, don't hesitate, Gina. You've been alone too long.'

Frowning, Gina said, 'There's more to life than having a man around, you know!'

'They help to make life more fun, though!' Hazel winked at her. 'Come on, admit it! They're a lot more exciting than a lonely cup of cocoa and a TV supper for one!'

Gina couldn't help a giggle.

Hazel grinned broadly. 'There you are, you know I'm right. Oh, I know how badly it hit you when your husband died, but you've got to start living again. Time doesn't stand still, you know.'

Gina was relieved when the telephone began to purr discreetly. She quickly picked it up. 'Hello? Oh, yes, she's here—yes, I'll send her through.'

Hazel mouthed 'Sir George?' and Gina nodded. Hazel hurried towards the door.

'Tell me all about that gorgeous guy later!' she threw over her shoulder.

'She's on her way now,' Gina said into the phone.

'You girls spend too much time gossiping!' Sir George said crossly. 'Whenever I want her, Hazel seems to be in your office!'

'I'm sorry,' Gina said gently. It wasn't true, Hazel was a very hard-working and efficient secretary who spent very little time out of her office, but the old man was on edge and irritated, so she did not argue or try to make him see how unfair he was being.

'So I should think! And I want you here, too, at once!' he snapped.

When she walked into his office she found it crowded with people—a circle of chairs had been placed around his desk. Everyone glanced round at her, their faces mostly familiar. Gina smiled politely and was given polite smiles in return. Hazel winked at her discreetly.

'Come and sit next to me, my dear,' Sir George said, gesturing to a chair which had been placed next to his, behind his desk.

Gina took the seat, hoping she looked calmer than she felt. It was nerve-racking to be seated so prominently. These people were all high-powered and imposing, whereas she knew she owed her place solely to the fact that she had married Sir George's grandson. But for that, the highest she would ever have reached was a job as a secretary.

'You all know my grandson's widow, Mrs Tyrrell,' Sir George said, patting her hand as he leaned back to contemplate the ring of faces. 'No doubt you've wondered why I have brought her into the firm, kept her near me. Well, she isn't here just because I like having her with me. She is all I have left in the world, my only family, and I want her to learn the business fast so that she'll be ready to take my place when I'm gone.'

There was an audible intake of breath from everyone in the room, and Gina turned white, her green eyes enormous as they met Hazel's startled grey ones.

Take his place? He couldn't be serious! What did he mean? That he was going to... leave his shares in the company to her? The very idea made her blood run cold. She had stayed with him after her husband died for a number of reasons—because he needed her, because she was lonely and unhappy, and not least because they had both loved James so much and his death made them instinctively cling together for comfort. Sir George had taken the place of the family she no longer had.

But however close she and the old man became it had never occurred to her that he might leave her his shares in the company. She had inherited some money from James, anyway. It was carefully invested and she had never touched it because she did not need much money. She lived luxuriously in Sir George's Mayfair house, and only spent money on clothes and personal items, which she paid for from her monthly salary. She had vaguely imagined Sir George would leave his company to a distant male relative, of which he had several, although he never saw them.

There were second cousins in Australia who had sent letters of condolence when James died, but they had not come to the funeral. Perhaps their polite indifference explained why Sir George didn't want to make them his heirs?

This was the first time that he had ever hinted that he might make her his heir, and the very prospect terrified her. She didn't want him to do it. Panic raced through her at the very idea. She could never cope with such a responsibility.

Still very pale and frowning, she looked up to find herself forgotten again. Sir George was talking about a new competition the *Sentinel* might be going to launch, another attempt to raise circulation figures and attract more advertising.

'I'm not sure our readers are interested in snooker!' he said to the marketing director, Bill Watson.

'We're always getting letters asking for more snooker reports,' said Bill, a short, stocky man with a bald head and bulging eyes. 'If you want the survey results, then...' he went on, and plunged into a series of statistics. He could talk a blue streak and Sir George soon looked dazed.

'Well, shall we see how other people feel?' he interrupted when Bill paused for breath. 'Can I have a show of hands? Who is for Bill's idea?'

Bill had convinced most people, hands went up and Sir George looked around, shrugging irritably.

'Very well, go ahead with it, then, Bill. Now, how are special features doing?'

'We're managing to come up with new ideas,' the special features editor quickly said. 'And the advertising is coming in very well.'

'Not fast enough,' said the advertising manager sourly. 'I think the well is running dry. Maybe you should look further afield for ideas—the Far East is a promising advertising area.'

The special features editor nodded. 'I'm ahead of you, and I happen to have...'

Gina looked out of the window at the livid sky. When would spring come? It seemed years since she had last seen the sun.

Half an hour later, Sir George went off to his club and Gina went down to the lobby to meet Roz, who attracted lots of attention in her black ski pants, white sweater and vivid red duffle coat. She looked like a boy, her body slim to the point of being skinny, and her jet-black hair worn very short, in wild disarray.

'You're late!' she told Gina tartly.

'Sorry, I was held up in an inter-departmental meeting. At least I managed to get a table at the Cheshire Cheese!'

Just as they reached the main door, leading into Fleet Street, someone tall and thin hurtled past them, almost knocking Roz down. Over his shoulder he muttered, '*Désolé*!' without looking.

'That's right, mow me down in the street,' Roz yelled after him, and his black head flicked round in recognition. He gave her a glinting grin.

The foreign news editor was not Roz's favourite man; Daniel Bruneille had a tongue like a razor and, under pressure, the personality of a scorpion. He was thought by many on the paper to be a brilliant foreign newsman, but he was a terror to his staff.

'What's your problem, *copine*?' he called back, his jet eyes mocking her, then he vanished at a run and Roz turned angry pink.

'If he calls me buddy one more time . . . !'

'Don't let him needle you!' Gina advised.

'Easy for you to say! You don't have to work with him.'

They dodged the traffic across the road to turn into the alley in which the pub could be found. Fleet Street was quite busy, but before the national newspapers began their exodus to other parts of London it had been far busier. London was changing radically year by year; two major landmarks had gone already, Covent Garden market and Fleet Street.

'I love your coat!' Roz said in a calmer tone.

Pleased, Gina smoothed down the collar. 'I bought it in Sweden when I went there with the old man last winter.' The ankle-length astrakhan swirled around her legs as she walked. 'It's very luxurious to wear!'

'It looks Russian.'

'Yes, doesn't it?'

The Cheshire Cheese was crowded, as usual, but they were shown to their table immediately, ordered drinks and read the menu.

'I can recommend the Olde English steak, kidney, mushroom and oyster pie,' Gina told Roz, who made a face.

'Much too heavy. No, I'll just have sole, grilled plain, please, no butter, and served with a salad.'

Gina had fish, too, but with hot vegetables, and they both started their meal with melon, and only drank mineral water. When the waiter had gone, Gina gave Roz a searching look, noticing a shadowy look around her eyes, a tension in the set of her mouth which was not normally there.

'You sounded odd on the phone—is something wrong, Roz?'

'Nothing I can't handle. And, anyway,' Roz said with a defiant look, 'I hate to broadcast my private life—makes me feel I'm starring in a TV soap opera.'

Gina laughed. 'Oh, I get it now! It's a man? You always are bad-tempered when you're in love, aren't you? I wonder why?'

Roz turned dark red. 'What rubbish! You do get some crazy ideas—and don't you start analysing me. Haven't you heard—Freud is dead?'

Carefully, Gina asked, 'Who is he, Roz? Do I know him?'

'Who, Freud? He was an old Viennese obsessed with sex,' Roz said crossly. 'Even you must have heard of him!'

Gina laughed, but although she knew Roz was trying to evade the issue, persisted, 'You know who I mean! Your new man!'

'He isn't,' Roz said curtly. 'Not new, and not my man.'

Gina frowned over that, puzzled. 'Not new? Does that mean you've known him for a long time? Do I know him too? But...who?' She mentally ran through all the men she knew on the newspaper. It must be someone on Foreign, she thought; and then her mouth parted in a gasp. 'You don't mean Daniel Bruneille?'

Roz was a scalding red by now, her vivid blue eyes glittering with fury. 'Are you out of your mind? Daniel Bruneille? I hate the very sight of him, always have, even though my father thought he was such a genius!'

'Did he?' Gina asked, looking interested. Maybe that was why Roz disliked Daniel so much—because her adored father had had such a high opinion of him? 'Well, Daniel is pretty good, isn't he?'

'Maybe,' said Roz angrily, 'But if he doesn't stop hassling me, some day I know I'll kill him.'

CHAPTER THREE

GINA slipped into the Greek restaurant just after eight o'clock, her skin flushed from walking quickly in the teeth of a howling gale. She was glad she didn't live by the sea, or near any big trees. On television that evening she had seen pictures of storm-lashed coasts and roads blocked by fallen oaks.

The weather hadn't made it any easier to leave the house without arousing Sir George's curiosity. She had had to lie, saying that she was meeting an old schoolfriend, and she was uneasy about that.

'Roz Amery?' he had asked, peering at her over the top of horn-rimmed spectacles.

'No, Patsy Wood,' she had said, remembering a girl in her class who had gone to New Zealand. 'You wouldn't know her, she's been abroad for years.'

The lie still sat in her throat as the Greek head waiter deftly removed her coat and handed it to a cloakroom attendant. 'Mr Caspian? Of course, *kyria*. This way.'

She almost fled at that instant, hating the guilt, the need for secrecy—but she couldn't go without her coat and she couldn't face asking for it back. So she followed the man through the crowded, softly lit room, to a discreet alcove, relieved at least not to recognise anyone or, so far as she could tell, be recognised.

'Your guest, Mr Caspian,' the head waiter said, bowing, and Nick rose to his feet.

'Good evening,' he said, looking into her eyes. She looked back, quite mesmerised by the way he looked in his smooth-fitting dark suit; blue-striped shirt and king-fisher-blue silk tie. He wasn't good-looking, she told herself yet again—but the trouble was, he was intensely sexy.

'Sorry I'm late,' she stammered as the head waiter pulled back a chair. She collapsed into it before her legs gave out.

'Would you like an aperitif, madam?'

She looked helplessly at him, not knowing what to order, and Nick Caspian intervened.

'Will you permit me to order something for you?' He began speaking deep, rapid Greek and the head waiter beamed.

'*Málista!*'

'What have you told him to bring me?' Gina ruefully asked as the man vanished.

'Nothing that will do you any harm!' Nick Caspian promised, but she looked at him with suspicious green eyes.

'I don't trust you!'

'I know you don't,' he said in that soft, mocking voice, and they were talking double-talk again. She never quite knew what he really meant, but she felt threatened, and that was what he wanted her to feel. Nick Caspian was good at making people feel uneasy; it was part of his technique for winning whatever game he was playing at the time, whether business or personal. He put you off balance and then he moved so fast you didn't have time to realise what was happening until too late.

Gina looked away, her brows meeting. Well, he wouldn't catch her off guard—she was forewarned.

A wine waiter appeared with a clear, golden-yellow drink on a tray and Nick watched her take a wary sip from the tall glass. It tasted good, she had to admit that, and it had a delicious scent, like a meadow on a summer day.

'What's in it?' she asked and Nick shrugged.

'White wine, herbs, honey. Do you like it?'

'Yes, thank you,' she said politely, accepting a menu from the head waiter. 'But I will order my own meal, if you don't mind,' she told Nick Caspian, who laughed.

'You know Greek food?'

'Yes,' Gina said offhandedly, skating a glance down the items on the menu. 'I'll have stuffed tomatoes, please, followed by lamb kebab with Greek salad and pitta bread.'

Nick ordered a rather more elaborate meal, chose a wine, and then the waiter disappeared, leaving them alone. The alcove was dimly lit and not overlooked by any other table. A tape of Greek music was playing just loudly enough to cover the buzz of conversation from other diners. Gina sipped some more of her aperitif, head bent.

'What did you tell Sir George?' he enquired drily and she looked up, grimacing.

'That I was meeting an old friend. I felt so uncomfortable! I hate lying to him. I'm sure I must have looked as guilty as I felt.'

'He probably thought you were meeting a lover,' Nick drawled, and she blushed, to her fury. It was a teenage habit she had never grown out of, and she hated it.

'That colour suits you,' he softly said, then, as her flush deepened, added in a teasing voice, 'I meant your dress, of course.'

He probably hadn't, but she said stiffly, 'Thank you.' She had spent an hour trying to decide what to wear and in the end had settled on a jade-green silk dress, the folds clinging softly to every contour of her body. It was simple and elegant, and the style and colour suited her.

He leaned across the table to gaze into her eyes. 'It makes your eyes a deeper green, too.'

He was flirting with her, but there was wicked amusement in his face because he knew she didn't want to play this sort of game. She looked down, and, a second later, the waiter arrived.

'Oh, our first course!' she said brightly, and Nick laughed under his breath.

'What a relief!'

She ignored the mockery, concentrating on her tomatoes baked with a filling of rice and herbs. Nick was eating an unfamiliar-looking fish with a smooth pink sauce poured around it.

'Did you enjoy your lunch with Roz Amery?' he asked suddenly a moment or two later, and she started, looking across the table in surprise.

'How do you know I had lunch with her?'

'Was it a secret?' he countered.

'No, of course not, but...' She did not like the way he seemed so knowledgeable about her and her life. Yesterday she had never even met the man! There was something almost diabolical about his omniscience. 'Do you know Roz?' she asked, and guessed in advance that he would say he did.

'I know her father, Desmond Amery, actually—he worked for me for a year, on one of my Italian papers.'

'How many newspapers do you own?' she asked, and he shrugged.

'Major national papers? Oh, twenty. I couldn't give a definite figure on the provincial ones—I keep acquiring them, the figure changes all the time.'

She absorbed that in silence while she ate, and Nick talked about Roz's famous father.

'He wanted to live in Rome for a while, to write a book about Italian politics since the war, and working for me, writing a column twice a week, paid for his living expenses while he was there. It was an amazing book, too—what was the title now?' He had finished his fish and was sipping his white wine, frowning while he thought. 'Oh, yes. *Italian Kaleidoscope*. Have you read it?'

She shook her head. 'I have read a couple of his books, but not that one.'

'He's a fine writer,' Nick said seriously. 'I was proud to have him working for me. He's always been a hero of mine. A Renaissance man, with many talents; a great journalist and writer, but he's more than that. He has a brilliant mind. I've always been in awe of him.'

'Roz is very proud of being his daughter,' Gina said, knowing that that was a simplification of how Roz felt. Pride was part of it, but being Desmond Amery's daughter was no easy matter.

Nick Caspian's mouth twisted. 'It must be hard to live up to, though,' he said, his own thought echoing hers.

The waiter appeared to whisk away their plates, and paused to refill their glasses.

'How did you know I had met Roz for lunch?' she asked Nick again, when the waiter had gone.

'There's nothing sinister about it—I happened to have lunch at the Press Club and bumped into Daniel Bruneille.'

Gina's eyes widened. 'Oh. . .' she said in an involuntary gasp, and Nick gave her a hard, probing look.

'Now, I wonder why his name should make you look so self-conscious?'

She felt herself flush again and crossly looked away. 'So it was Daniel who told you I was meeting Roz?'

'It was,' Nick said curtly. 'How well do you know him?'

'How do you know Daniel?' she retorted, wondering if it could be Daniel who was feeding him inside information about the *Sentinel*. But would Daniel Bruneille do that? She couldn't believe it. She'd swear that Daniel had integrity; a burning, icy integrity which was made up of pride, a certain arrogance which many Frenchmen seemed to have quite naturally, and an independent sense of himself and his own worth. Daniel Bruneille wouldn't sell out his employer, it would lower his opinion of himself.

In his thirties, very thin and fast-moving, with curly dark hair, a smooth olive skin and sharp black eyes, he had been born in Montreal of a French family and had grown up bilingual, which perhaps had given him a head start, because eventually he had learned to speak nine languages more or less fluently. Daniel had a mind like a razor, and spoke that mind forcefully. Explosively passionate in argument, highly charged with energy, he had always been a committed European, fascinated by other countries, and had been an award-winning foreign correspondent himself for years before settling down behind the foreign news editor's desk in London.

'I know Daniel because he worked for me in Paris,' Nick drawled. 'He only stayed a year, and I only met him once at that time, at an international conference, but it was obvious from the start that he had star quality, and I've kept my eye on him ever since in the hope of luring him back.' He gave her another hard stare, those grey eyes piercing. 'Have you?'

Bewildered, she said, 'What?'

'Got your eye on him.'

'Will you stop asking me personal questions?' she flared crossly. What on earth had made him think she was interested in Daniel? Not that she would deny it; she wouldn't give him the satisfaction. He kept hinting that there hadn't been a man in her life since James died, which she resented all the more because it was true. He was not implying that she was frustrated or weird!

The waiter arrived with their second course. It was beautifully presented and tasted as good as it looked. The lamb was meltingly tender, the crisp green salad sprinkled with fetta cheese delicious.

Neither of them said anything much while they ate, but when the waiter had removed their plates again and given them the dessert list to study Nick coolly said, 'I've been watching Roz Amery, too, with considerable interest, so I asked Daniel what he thought of her work since she joined the foreign desk on the *Sentinel*, which is why he happened to tell me she was having lunch with you today.'

'Daniel didn't want her on the foreign desk, did he tell you that?' Gina broke out, and Nick nodded, his mouth wry.

'He mentioned it, yes. He didn't think she was experienced enough, or old enough, for a job as foreign correspondent.'

'That's just an excuse. He didn't want her for other reasons. Firstly, because she is a woman, and Daniel doesn't think the foreign desk is a job for a woman—it isn't safe enough.'

'There's something in that,' Nick said mildly.

'I don't agree! Roz has worked abroad for five years!'

'In pretty safe countries like France,' Nick pointed out.

'She has lived all over the world. She has always been on the foreign side, and, after all, she travelled around with her father for years. In any case, these days there are lots of women foreign correspondents. No, his real reason for wanting to keep her out is because he and Roz have never hit it off. And now that she knows he tried to block her job, she likes him a whole lot less.'

'He worked with Desmond in Montreal and again in Paris,' Nick said. 'He always talks about him with reverence, but I wouldn't be surprised if he thinks Roz Amery has used her father as a springboard to launch her own career, and resents it.'

'It isn't true, anyway! Roz has worked like mad to get where she is; she deserves that job.'

Nick smiled at her vehemence. 'I'm sure she does.'

Flushed, Gina admitted, 'I admire the way she has built her career so single-mindedly. It hasn't been easy, if that is what Daniel thinks. Her mother died when she was small, and her father had to leave her in boarding-school in England once she was old enough. That was where I met her, we were in the same class and we had both lost our mothers. It made a bond between us.'

'I imagine it did,' he said, watching her intently, as if he was really interested.

Gina had forgotten her distrust of him. She smiled wryly. 'I remember how she used to vanish every summer, to join her father in whatever part of the world he was covering at that time. We all envied her like mad, it seemed a very glamorous way of life, globe-trotting and visiting war zones and trouble spots. My father worked for Sir George on the *Sentinel*, but he was an accountant, he wasn't a reporter, and we never left London except for brief holidays in France or Spain.'

'Is that how you met your husband?' Nick asked, watching her acutely. 'Because your father worked for his grandfather?'

She looked away, into the distance, her green eyes searching for the memory. It had used to be so sharp, so clear, but now it grew mistier all the time, receding into oblivion. She had thought she would never forget an instant of that evening, and it was painful to admit how little of it she could now recall.

'We met at the annual Christmas dinner-dance for the *Sentinel* staff. They held it at a Park Lane hotel, in a gold and cream ballroom, with giant chandeliers glittering overhead—it was very glamorous. James went that year, for the first time, and so did I.'

They had been the same age, both very young, drawn to each other instantly because of their youth, ill at ease among the throngs of journalists, secretaries, photographers, advertising men—all older and seeming sure of themselves, sophisticated.

'A romantic occasion!' Nick's cynical voice broke in on that vanished dream, startling her.

'Yes, it was!' she threw back defiantly. He wasn't patronising her or sneering at her memories. She had married James because she loved him and they had been happy together—Nick Caspian didn't seem to be either the romantic or the marrying kind, he just dated glossy beautiful Swedish models, like the girl photographed with him in a newspaper yesterday. Or maybe he was already married, and Christa Nordstrom was his mistress?

'Are you married?' she asked impulsively, and then bit her lip, her colour deepening.

His glance was amused. 'Now I wonder what made you ask that? No, I'm not, so you can stop worrying.'

'Who's worrying?' she said crossly, but at the back of her mind she was wondering exactly what sort of relationship he had with the beautiful Swedish model. Was it serious, had it been going on for long?

'How old are you?' he asked, openly mocking, and still watching her with his gleaming, amused grey eyes. Without waiting for her to answer he asked, 'How old were you when you got married?'

She glared. 'Mr Caspian, I don't know why we keep talking about my private life...'

'You were talking about mine!' he teased, and she snapped back.

'Well, can we get on with talking about business? You said you wanted to talk about Sir George's financial problems, so can we do that?'

The waiter arrived at that moment, and Nick coolly ordered Greek coffee for them both. The man hurried away, and Nick leaned back in his chair, his hands resting on the white tablecloth, studying her as if curious to understand what made her tick. She stared back at him, waiting with impatience, and some uneasiness, for whatever he was going to say.

At last he leaned towards her, his grey eyes brilliant, hypnotic, under that sleek black hair which capped his head.

'I can solve Sir George's money worries at a stroke,' he said. 'Of course, ideally, I would like to buy his ma-

jority share-holding in the *Sentinel*, the whole fifty-one
per cent—which would give me full control immediately.'

Gina drew an appalled breath, but he was still talking.

'Then I could inject new capital into the firm, pay off
the bank loan, underwrite the move to Barbary Wharf
and weather any time-lag between leaving the old Fleet
Street building and selling it.'

'So he was right!' Gina bitterly broke out. 'The old
man said you were a ruthless swine——'

He put a hand lightly over her mouth and she almost
bit it.

'Let go of me!' she mumbled behind the muffling
palm.

'Wait a minute, before you call me all the names under
the sun,' he said brusquely, his grey eyes unsmiling now.

She glared at him angrily, as he went on.

'I said that would be my ideal solution, but I realise
Sir George isn't likely to agree, so instead I'm offering
a compromise, a face-saving agreement where I inject
capital and am given a seat on the board, with a strong
voice in future policy, and the right to make a few management changes in the staff.'

Gina stared at him uncertainly, and he dropped the
hand silencing her, and raised one dark brow enquiringly.

'Well? Do you think he would go for that?'

'Are you serious?' she slowly asked, searching his hard
face for reassurance. 'I mean, is this an offer you want
me to put to Sir George?'

'That's why I asked you to meet me,' he assured her.
'Will you act as go-between? Sir George is like a dog
sitting on a thistle at the moment; he's hurting but he
is too stubborn to shift. You can reach him, I think he'll

listen to you. So yes, that is my offer, and I'll wait with interest to hear if he is ready to talk about it.'

The waiter arrived and poured them each a small cup of strong Greek coffee heavily laced with sugar. It tasted like sweet mud, and Gina sipped it warily. A little of it would go a long way.

When they were alone again, Nick said quietly, 'And you can rest assured that that is an honest statement of intent. I've put everything up front. My accountants and lawyers would shudder if they heard me.'

'How do I know I can trust you, Mr Caspian——?' she began, and he interrupted.

'Isn't it time you started calling me Nick?'

Her green eyes wavered. 'We only met today!'

'Was it only today?' His voice had lowered, become husky and intimate, and she felt a little shiver run up her spine. That thought had occurred to her once or twice. Had they really only known each other for a few hours?

'Yes,' she said huskily. 'I don't know much about you, Mr Caspian, but I'm not blind or stupid and, for all your talk about being frank, isn't it true that your long-term goal is to push Sir George out of his own company and take it over yourself?'

'That was my original intention,' he admitted.

'That makes you his enemy!' she muttered.

His grey eyes narrowed. 'And makes you mine?'

'I love the old man very much,' she said obliquely.

'His friends are your friends, and his enemies are your enemies?' he murmured, his mouth twisting. 'You have a strong instinct for loyalty, don't you? I hope the old man realises what sort of ally he has in you! That is what you call him inside your head, isn't it? The old man. Several times you've let it slip out. And you're right—he is an old man, a very old man, and he's getting past the age when he should be running a major company.'

He was very persuasive, but she argued back, 'He isn't the managing director—he is only chairman of the board, he doesn't deal with the day-to-day running of the company or the newspaper. Joe Mackinlay is managing director.'

'Sir George's yes-man?' Nick Caspian dismissed with a derisive shrug. 'You know very well that he is just there to do the dull work. He's a solid workhorse with very little imagination. Keeps the paper ticking over, knows the routine like the back of his hand—but has no flair and no instinct. Sir George may have given him the title but he hasn't given him the power. He keeps that in his own hands, as he always has. He has the majority shareholding, the company is run his way, and he picks all the men who ostensibly run it.'

It was only too true—but how did he know so much?

'Who is your spy in the *Sentinel*, Mr Caspian?' she angrily asked. 'Do you know what Sir George said to me about you? He called you an octopus with tentacles everywhere—and he was right, wasn't he? I've only known you a few hours but I have already discovered how ruthless you are. You're paying someone to tell you the *Sentinel*'s secrets.'

'Am I?' He considered her across the table, his strong face speculative. 'What makes you think so?'

'You do, Mr Caspian,' she said scornfully. 'You've been boasting to me about your wide contacts in the newspaper business. You know everybody, you told me,

even on the *Sentinel*. Roz and her father, Daniel and Joe
Mackinlay, for a start! Is one of them your spy?'

'You have a very melodramatic mind!' he mocked,
and her flush deepened.

'Maybe, but you've admitted that you never lose sight
of anyone you meet who might be useful to you, even
when they are living in another continent! I think you
use people. So who on the *Sentinel* is selling us out?'

'A small world, the newspaper business!' he told her
coolly, without denying any of her accusations. 'People
in our trade move around a good deal. They never stay
on one paper forever, and they don't even stay in one
country for long. They move on a well-worn circuit, from
Europe to the States and back, from Australia to Hong
Kong and on to England. It's part of their make-up—
restless and footloose. Every spring they start reading
the trade papers to look for a new job, the grass always
seems greener somewhere else, and, if they are good, or
even if they're not, it isn't hard to switch jobs. Any good
proprietor—and I am a good one, I won't be modest
about it—keeps an eye out for talent and never forgets
a name worth remembering. What is wrong with that?'

'It sounds wonderful,' she scornfully said. 'But what
it means is, you use people. You're trying to use me now.
I'm not stupid. I know what you're doing. And I won't
let you use me to get at the old man. I don't trust you,
or your offer of a compromise. I think that what you
really want is to get your foot in the door, and then slowly
but surely force yourself right inside. And then, God
help anyone in your way. You would crush the old man
without a second's hesitation. Well, I won't help you do
it.'

She got to her feet, almost upsetting the table, and walked away, leaving her syrupy black coffee half drunk. The cloakroom attendant found her coat just as Nick Caspian caught up with her. She had hoped he would be delayed in paying the bill, but no doubt he had merely signed it.

Wordlessly, he took her coat from the waiter and held it while she slid her arms into the sleeves, very aware of him standing right behind her but managing to avert her face and maintain an icy silence.

The waiter opened the door and she walked out almost blundering into someone just arriving. 'Sorry,' she muttered without looking at them, and then froze.

'Hello, Gina. Haven't seen you for ages,' said the woman she had bumped into and whom Gina had recognised with a sinking heart. Heavily made-up, the face belonged to a spry, attenuated woman of about fifty with silvery, curling hair, a fine set of pearly dentures and a short mink jacket. 'I was talking to George this evening,' she was chattering in her very middle-class English voice, 'inviting him to a party I'm giving on Saturday evening—come along, too, won't you?' While she spoke her eyes were busy over Gina's shoulder, taking in the man behind her.

'Thank you, Laura, I'll let you know,' Gina said jaggedly, trying to walk past, but Laura Dailey was determined not to move out of the way or let her escape yet.

Sir George called her 'the Merry Widow' and it suited her; she had lost her husband some five years ago and had been enjoying life at top speed ever since. She had endless parties, was always to be seen at first nights or

film premières and loved the latest successful res-
taurants, which was why she was here, tonight.

'Who is this you have with you?' she asked, without
waiting for a reply. 'Nick Caspian, isn't it?' And she
gave him a smile as bright as the beam of a lighthouse.

'That's right,' Nick drawled, looking amused. 'Aren't
you going to introduce your lovely friend, Gina?'

Laura loved that. She offered him a heavily ringed
hand. 'I like you already, Mr Caspian—or may I call
you Nick?'

'Please do, Laura,' he said with smooth flattery, and
Gina angrily wondered why Laura Dailey could not hear
the insincerity in every word. Of course, she loved it too
much to want to think about whether he meant it.

But Gina hated listening to him because everything he
said underlined for her the absolute impossibility of
trusting him. If he could lay siege to Laura Dailey
without scruple, how could *she* believe a word he said?

'Have you been eating here? Is it as good as the advance publicity says it is?' Laura fluttered her thickly
mascaraed lashes up at him, still clasping his hand.

'It's excellent, he said. 'We enjoyed the food, didn't
we, Gina?'

She didn't answer, her profile rigidly turned away.

Laura gave a tinkling little giggle. 'Sir George did tell
me you were dining out with an old school-friend, Gina!'

She felt Nick's mocking eyes and didn't look in his
direction. 'He was mistaken,' she said stiffly to Laura,
who gave another giggle.

'I can see that, naughty girl! Oh, don't worry, I won't
breathe a word. Your secret is safe with me.'

Her escort, a soldierly man in his sixties, cleared his throat rather crossly. 'Getting chilly standing around out here, m'dear—better get inside, don't you think?'

'Yes, darling, I'm coming,' Laura cooed, gave Nick Caspian another alluring smile and invited, 'Get Gina to bring you to my party on Saturday, or come along without her if she can't make it. I live in Farthing Court, two streets from here. The first floor apartment, you'll find it easily enough. Saturday night, eight o'clock onwards, drop in any time. We'll go on for hours.'

Then she was gone and Gina furiously walked towards the corner, relieved that she would very soon be safely back home. Nick caught up with her in a couple of long-legged strides, she felt his sideways glance, the amusement in his eyes, and resented it.

'Charming woman,' he said.

'Yes, just your type,' Gina bit out, and he gave her a sharp look.

'Ouch. That was nasty.'

'You deserve it.'

'You really don't like her, do you?' he said.

Bitterly Gina told him, 'I hope she starts ringing you up day and night, the way she does Sir George. It isn't easy to shake Laura Dailey off once she has her hooks into you!'

'Is she chasing Sir George?' he asked, raising one lazy eyebrow in amusement.

'She chases every man she meets.' Gina was walking very fast as she came in sight of the double-fronted Edwardian house in which she and Sir George lived. It was spacious, elegant, with stucco on the façade, and two smooth white pillars supporting a portico.

She could see a light in Sir George's bedroom window.
He would be in bed by now, since it was gone ten o'clock
and when he dined at home he always went to bed early.
He still lived by the old maxim: 'early to bed, early to
rise makes a man healthy, wealthy and wise'. He was
always up by seven and often at his desk in the office
by eight, except when he went down to Barbary Wharf
to view the progress of the building work.

'Why are you so angry?' Nick abruptly asked,
grabbing her arm and forcing her to halt.

She tilted her head back to glare at him. 'Mr Caspian,
I have had enough of your company for one day. From
the minute I set eyes on you I was sure I didn't like you,
and now I just want to get home and forget I ever met
you.'

His face tightened as if she had hit him. Gina wrenched
her arm free and ran, and this time Nick Caspian did
not follow her.

In her bedroom, though, she lay awake for a long time
in troubled uneasiness. She didn't imagine for a moment
that he was going to give up his assault on the *Sentinel*.
Having failed to persuade her to help him, no doubt he
would find someone else to do what he wanted. Nick
Caspian was a tough and ruthless enemy, and he was
accustomed to winning.

She told herself she hated him, and it was true—but
like most things it was not that simple. She hated him
for what he wanted to do to the old man but she couldn't
stop thinking about him. She hated him for lying to her
and trying to use her, but whenever she remembered his
husky voice, the crooked charm of his sudden smile, she
felt her heart turn over.

CHAPTER FOUR

GINA didn't attend the board meeting, but, while she and Hazel worked on some letters which had to go out that morning, she kept looking anxiously at the clock. This was the longest board meeting she could remember. What was going on in the oak-panelled boardroom at the far end of this floor? She had helped Hazel get the room ready, aware all the time of the paintings of earlier Tyrrells on the walls; whiskered and important, staring down at her arrogantly. They were not a charming bunch, she had thought, but they had such inviolable confidence!

'What's on your mind?' Hazel asked her, and she started.

'What did you say?'

'You keep staring at your watch. Are you expecting an exciting phone call?'

'No, I'm not!' Gina said, flushing.

'Are you still seeing him?'

'I don't know what you're talking about!' lied Gina, although she knew perfectly well that Hazel meant Nick Caspian. She had not seen him for a week—since the night they had dinner at the Knossos. She kept telling herself she was glad he had got the message, and was leaving her alone, but he was always in her mind, haunting her. She barely knew the man, and what she did know about him she didn't like—so why couldn't she forget him?

'Oh, come off it! You know very well who I mean,' Hazel grinned, not taken in by her blank expression. 'What did you say his name was?'

'I didn't,' Gina said shortly. 'Can we get on with our work? It will be lunchtime soon.'

'Is it that late?' Hazel looked at her watch. 'The board meeting should be over by now—whatever can those men find to talk about? They've been in there for hours!'

Gina couldn't stop an involuntary sigh, and Hazel gave her a sharp look.

'What's wrong, Gina? You know, there is a lot of gossip going around——'

'You shouldn't listen!'

Hazel stiffened at the angry note in Gina's voice. However friendly she might be, it was impossible to forget that Gina was one of the Tyrrells. Gina never forgot it herself. If she felt you had stepped over some invisible line, she would slap you down at once.

'I always tell them it's irresponsible, spreading alarmist talk,' Hazel said rather coldly. 'I don't encourage gossip!'

Gina gave her a quick, apologetic look. 'Oh, I'm sorry, Hazel. I didn't mean to snap, it's just that I'm worried...'

Hazel relented, watching her. She often felt very sorry for Gina. However luxurious her surroundings, she must be lonely at times, living in that great house alone with a very old man who wasn't even her own flesh and blood. She was still very young; she shouldn't be living that way.

'I know,' Hazel soothed. 'The company is having its problems, you can't be surprised about that in the circumstances—all the trouble there has been down at Barbary Wharf, the time it has taken to build! The Pharaohs built the Pyramids faster! I know Sir George is worried about the cost, he keeps having meetings with the accountants and lawyers, and it's obvious there are money worries, but long-term the company is solid and everyone's jobs are safe.'

Sir George had kept her in the dark, too, just as he had Gina. He had carried the burden of this worry all by himself, and he would not want her to give Hazel so much as a hint that the gossip was true.

'I'm sure you're right,' Gina said, thinking that even if the worst came to the worst a highly trained and efficient secretary like Hazel would have no problem getting another job. In fact, whoever took over the *Sentinel* would probably find her very useful. Bitterly, Gina wondered how Hazel would look if she had told her that it was on the cards that one day she might find herself working for Nick Caspian. She obviously found him very attractive.

Hazel gave a cheerful grin. 'Well, I'm glad about that! I hate gloom-merchants!'

Then Sir George walked in slowly, leaning on his stick. Gina gave him a hurried, searching look, alarmed by his pallor and the drawn lines of his face.

'Meeting over at last? They get longer all the time,' Hazel said happily, collecting up her pile of letters.

'Yes,' he said bleakly. 'Gina, get me a small tumbler of whisky, will you?'

The two girls exchanged looks, but Gina did not argue.

Hazel said brightly, 'You have a lunch appointment in half an hour, with those people from the Shelton Trust. I've left a list of important phone calls on your desk, here. None of them needed an urgent reply, but the top three do want an answer some time today. Is there anything you want me to do before lunch, Sir George?'

He shook his head and sank into his padded leather chair, a hand held out for the tumbler of whisky Gina brought him. Hazel discreetly left, closing the door behind her, and Gina stood beside the old man, putting a hand on his shoulder in a comforting gesture.

'What happened?'

'It was the most difficult meeting I've ever chaired,' he muttered. 'Listening to them, you'd think I'd deliberately set out to destroy the company. Well, it's typical, I suppose. They're scared; most of them have shares in the firm and are afraid of losing their money. But I appointed every one of them to the board, you know. I thought some of them were my friends. It seems you can't trust anyone. I wouldn't be surprised if they aren't all on the phone to Nick Caspian today.'

She blenched, and said bitterly, 'Rats deserting the sinking ship?'

Sir George gave her a glare. 'We aren't sinking yet! Don't you start writing us off, too!'

'No,' she said, horrified. 'Of course not, I only meant...'

The old man patted her hand, sighing. 'I know, I know...sorry, my dear, my temper is very short at the moment. These men come along to board meetings and only want to rubber-stamp decisions, and then when things get tough they turn on you.'

'Was any decision made this time?' she asked.

'A shareholders' meeting is to be called at once,' he gruffly said, then drained his tumbler and set it down on the desk with a small thud.

His eye fell on the list of telephone calls Hazel had left on his desk. 'I see Laura rang again!'

'Ignore her,' Gina advised.

'I can't risk annoying her at the moment. She holds five per cent of the voting stock.'

Gina hadn't realised that. Frowning, she wondered— had Nick Caspian known? Was that why he had been so surprisingly charming to Laura? She knew how someone like him operated, getting hold of a list of shareholders, checking up on them to see if any were likely to sell. If he realised Laura owned shares in the *Sentinel*, he would probably take her up on the invitation to her party and talk her into selling.

'Are you going to her party on Saturday?' she asked the old man, who groaned.

'I suppose I must—that's probably why she's ringing, to remind me again.'

Gina bit her lower lip. If he went, and Nick was there, Laura might maliciously let slip the fact that she had seen Nick and Gina at the Knossos. She was that sort of woman; she might have promised not to say anything, but she could be spiteful. It might be wiser to get in first, be frank about why she had met him secretly.

'Caspian is in the market, buying any shares that come up,' Sir George said wearily. 'He declared his interest this morning, and of course that has pushed the price of the shares up at once, and no doubt a lot of people will jump in to sell while they have the chance.' A bitter look crossed his face. 'Including members of our board, no doubt! Our price has been low for months. Now it is rising, they'll think that this is their chance to get rid of the shares while someone is ready to pay a good price for them.'

He leaned back in his chair, closing his eyes, and she looked at him with love and pity, wishing there was something she could do to help him.

Bleakly, he said, 'We've had rotten luck; we started to build Barbary Wharf at the wrong time in the economic cycle. If we had built it when things were on an upswing, we would have been fine, but how was I to guess recession would set in a couple of years after I made the decision to move?'

'Of course you couldn't guess! It's just bad luck,' she said quickly, then asked, 'Have you heard any more from Nick Caspian?'

'Oh, yes. He has requested a meeting—I didn't speak to him, but I got a long letter by courier. He seems to be hinting at some sort of deal...'

Gina took a deep breath and said huskily, 'I talked to him.'

The old man stared. 'What? When?'

'The other day,' she said.

Frowning, the old man demanded, 'On the phone?' She began to shake her head and he bit out, 'Did he come here again? Why didn't you tell me?'

'He asked me to...to act as a sort of go-between...to talk to you and suggest a compromise.' She saw the dark colour rising in the old man's face, the anger and shock, and hurriedly went on, 'I thought it might help if I talked to him, found out what he was planning, so...so I had dinner with him.'

'You did what?' he roared, and she flinched.

'I'm sorry if I was wrong, but I was only trying to help. He said that all he wanted was a seat on the board and a voice in policy-making. You would still be chairman.'

'Generous of him!' Sir George's brows were pleated, his eyes hard with concentration. 'That wouldn't satisfy him. This is just an opening move. He wants control, I know he does.' He gave her a fierce look, bristling. 'How could you agree to talk to him behind my back? I thought that you, of all people, would never betray me...'

'I didn't, I wouldn't,' she stammered, turning pale.

'It's bad enough that men I've known for years, men I invited on to the board myself, should turn on me,' he muttered, breathing thickly. 'But you! I never thought you would!'

Tears welled up in her green eyes. 'You can't believe I would ever do anything to hurt you!'

'You have hurt me,' he said. 'Go on, get out of my sight!'

She stood there, staring at him, distraught, and he banged his fist down on his desk, dark blue veins standing out on his temples. 'Go on, get out and leave me alone!'

She turned shakily to go, a sob in her throat, but as she got to the door he said roughly, 'No, no, I'm sorry, my dear. Of course I know you wouldn't betray me. You were right to talk to him; thank you for trying to help.'

She turned, tears running down her face, and he held out a blue-veined, trembling hand.

'I'm a stupid old man, my dear. Forgive me.'

She ran back and knelt beside his chair, leaning her head against him. He put his arm around her and patted her clumsily.

'Don't cry like that, you know I hate it when you cry.'

She half laughed, and he pushed a clean white handkerchief into her hand. 'Here, wipe your eyes and blow your nose.'

She obeyed and got up, knowing she must look a total mess now—all her make-up gone and her eyes red.

'I feel lost, Gina,' the old man said. 'I can't explain...but my will is paralysed, I don't know what to do. I keep watching disaster coming closer and closer and I can't do a thing to save myself, or the company. What am I going to do?'

Gently, she said, 'You could try talking to Nick Caspian. It wouldn't hurt, would it? You can always say no.'

There was a long silence, then he said, 'You're right, of course. I have to go to lunch with these charity people now—will you get in touch with Caspian and set up a meeting this afternoon? I should be free by three o'clock. The fewer people who know about the meeting the better, so tell him to meet me at our home, at three-fifteen—and you had better be there, Gina. It might be wiser if I had a witness. I'll go straight there after lunch. Meet me there just before three.' He looked at his watch. 'I must go. Caspian's telephone number is on his letter—you'll find it in the files. Insist on speaking to him personally; if he isn't there leave a message for him to ring you back. I want this kept very private.' He started slowly towards the door, then paused and looked back at her with a wry little smile. 'I am sorry I shouted at you, Gina.'

'You're under a terrible strain,' she said. 'I understood.'

When he had gone she went in search of the letter from Nick Caspian, then sat looking at the telephone as if it might bite her.

It took an effort of will to lift the receiver and start to dial. He probably wouldn't be there. He would be out at lunch by now, or busy. The number, she discovered, was that of a London office. 'Caspian International!' a woman's voice softly purred.

'Mr Caspian, please,' Gina said huskily.

'Who is speaking?' the calm voice enquired without interest, and she hesitated, then gave her name.

'Hold the line, please. I will see if Mr Caspian is available.'

Gina prayed he would not be there, but a moment later his deep voice said coolly, 'Hello?'

'Mr Caspian?' she asked, although she knew perfectly well that it was him because her heartbeat was running so fast that she was deafened.

'You know it is,' he said drily. 'What do you want, Gina?'

His tone made her angry, and there was ice in her voice as she said, 'Sir George would like to talk to you. Could you meet him at his home at three-fifteen this afternoon?'

A pause, then he said abruptly, 'This is very short notice.'

'Can't you make it?' She tried to sound as offhand as he did.

Another little silence, then he said, 'Oh, yes, I'll be there. What sort of meeting is this? Should I bring any of my people with me? Accountants, lawyers...?'

'No, Sir George wants this to be a private meeting— just you and him. He would rather you didn't tell anyone you were seeing him, either.'

'Just the two of us, then?' Nick sounded thoughtful; she could imagine the calculating look in those hard grey eyes, the swift workings of that very clever mind. He would be trying to guess what Sir George had decided to do.

'No,' she said with cold hostility. 'I'll be there, too, as a witness to your discussions.'

Mockery sounded in his voice. 'Two against one? Not very fair odds, but I accept. See you later, Gina.'

The phone went dead in her hand and she slowly put it down. She was trembling, and that made her even angrier. She must not let him get to her like this.

She was doing her make-up in the powder-room when Hazel came into the room and smiled. 'Ready?'

'More or less,' Gina said, and, while she waited, Hazel ran a comb through her hair and renewed her lipstick, gilding the lily as usual. She was always perfect, immaculate, looking as though she had just come from the hands of a beautician. Her work was the same: whatever she did was done with cool efficiency; she had to be the perfect secretary.

They took a bus to the West End of town. Today the sun had chosen to shine and London was getting ready for Christmas; the shop windows glittered in the wintry sunlight, gay with tinsel and Christmas trees, and Christmas decorations swung from one side of Oxford Street to the other.

'Looks lovely, doesn't it?' Hazel said, gazing out with a happy smile. 'I do love Christmas.'

'It's weeks away yet! Why do they start so early? It seems to start earlier every year.'

'Scrooge!' said Hazel as they got off the bus.

Oxford Street was packed with hurrying shoppers, but despite the sunlight there was a chilly wind and Gina shivered inside her Russian coat. Ever since she met Nick Caspian, she seemed to be having to live with one skin less. She was becoming ultra-sensitive to everything that happened, from the weather to an argument in the office.

Tears were never far away, and she was experiencing wild mood swings every day. It was disturbing.

They walked down one side of the street visiting all the shoe shops and just before they got to Marble Arch they found what Hazel was looking for—pale blue shoes to match a dress she had just bought for a friend's wedding.

'Where shall we eat?' Hazel asked.

'Selfridges?' suggested Gina as they were right outside the store, glancing at her watch. 'I haven't much time. I have to meet someone at three, so I'll have to leave you by half-past two.'

'OK by me,' said Hazel, and they took a lift up to the top floor. As they hovered at the door a waiter came over and told them apologetically that there were no free tables.

'Shall we wait?' Hazel asked, but Gina shook her head, turning away.

A voice behind them said, 'Hello again! Mrs Tyrrell— remember me? Piet van Leyden? I heard the waiter say that there are no free tables, but it would make me happy if you share my table. I am alone, but my table could easily seat three.'

Startled, she managed a shy smile. 'Thank you, Mr van Leyden, that's very kind.'

'Piet, please!'

'Oh, well, thank you, Piet—and I'm Gina.' She introduced Hazel, and he shook hands without really looking at her.

'How do you do?' he asked politely, then smiled at Gina. 'I didn't think I would ever have the luck to meet you again—this is wonderful. Do sit here.' The waiter had already laid two more places, while they were talking.

Piet ushered Gina into a chair next to his, Hazel sat on the other side of her, and the waiter handed them each a menu.

Catching Hazel's obviously enquiring eye, Gina explained, 'Mr van Leyden is an architect who works for Caspian International.'

'An architect?' Hazel repeated politely. 'How interesting.'

Piet gave her a brief look, another polite smile. 'Yes, I like it.'

Hazel was slightly flushed. She was very attractive, and accustomed to getting plenty of male attention; she was offended by Piet's lack of interest in her. 'Of course,' she said with belligerence, 'I'm just a secretary, nothing very interesting or important about me.' Was it the way Gina looked that he liked—or Sir George's money? she was wondering acidly.

'Hazel is being modest, she is Sir George Tyrrell's secretary,' Gina quickly said, trying to soothe her friend down a little.

Piet was not impressed. He smiled perfunctorily. 'Ah, really?'

'Yes, really,' Hazel snapped, her chin up.

Piet was already gazing at Gina again. 'And you are his personal assistant, is this not so?' he asked her, and she nodded, uneasy because of the furious glitter of Hazel's steel-grey eyes.

'You have been shopping?' Piet asked.

'I have,' Hazel curtly said. 'I bought some shoes.'

He spared her a fleeting look, perhaps hearing the anger in her tone. 'Oh? How nice,' he said with a brief pretence of interest, then his eyes were drawn back to Gina. 'And you? You did not buy anything?'

After that, Hazel lapsed into silence, brooding. Gina kept giving her worried looks. Piet van Leyden was making it plain that as far as he was concerned three was a crowd and he wished Hazel were not with them. Gina was embarrassed by that, but what could she do?

Luckily, the service was fast. Piet talked to Gina exclusively; she kept trying to include Hazel but Hazel wouldn't play ball. She ate the melon and grilled sole both girls had ordered, staring fixedly at her plate, and when she had finished, got to her feet.

'I'm off now, Gina. See you back in the office.'

Piet van Leyden glanced up, as if becoming aware of the hostility beamed in his direction. And then he made the biggest mistake he had made so far. He smiled warmly.

'Oh, you are leaving us?' he said, making no secret of the fact that that made him very happy.

'You bet I am!' Hazel snapped, turned on her heel and walked out. Piet van Leyden's vivid blue eyes opened wide, and he stared after her, apparently baffled.

'I said something wrong?' he asked Gina, forehead wrinkled.

She regarded him rather pityingly. 'It doesn't matter.' What was the point of explaining? He would probably never meet Hazel again, and if he did Hazel could get her own message home, as no doubt she would.

'A funny girl, your friend!' he said, then flashed her one of his charming, boyish smiles. 'But now that she is gone, there are just the two of us—now we can really get to know one another.'

Ruefully, Gina looked at her watch. 'I'm sorry, I shall have to leave too, in a moment.'

He sighed, the wintry sunlight through a nearby window turning his smooth blond head a gleaming gold. He was really almost beautiful, for a man, she thought, watching him. He had charm and warmth and was intensely likeable. He didn't have the dramatic force of Nick Caspian, of course. Heat kindled in her face. Nick wasn't the only sexy man in the world!

'I want to see you again,' he said, taking her hand. 'Please? Dinner, next time? We would have more time to talk.'

'One evening, maybe,' she said, signalling to the waiter. 'The bill for myself and the other lady, please.'

'No! I invited you to join me; I will pay the bill!' Piet said.

She didn't argue because she could see he was determined, and she didn't have time for a long discussion. Gina knew when to give in gracefully, so she smiled at him. 'Thank you, you're very kind,' she said, getting up. 'But now I must go, I'm afraid.'

'May I ring you?' he asked, rising too.

She hesitated, then on impulse said, 'Yes, of course.' Perhaps Piet was exactly the diversion she needed to stop herself thinking about Nick?

His eyes brightened. 'I shall look forward to that very much.'

As she hurried out of Selfridges and into a taxi she was lucky enough to pick up right outside, she wondered if he would mention their meeting to Nick? She hoped so.

When she got back to Sir George's house, well before three, she found it empty. Their housekeeper, Daphne, was probably out shopping, and her husband, John, would be driving Sir George. The two of them ran the household; Daphne cooked as well as cleaning the house, and John was not only the chauffeur but a general handyman.

Gina went through the hall to the back of the house where the kitchen lay behind tall, baize-lined mahogany doors. She made preparations for a pot of tea which she would serve when Sir George and Nick Caspian arrived, unless they asked for something else, then she ran upstairs to her bedroom to change her quiet dark grey skirt and elegant white shirt for something a little less subdued.

Not, of course, for Nick's benefit! she told herself. Well, not exactly. She still hated the man, and if she never saw him again that was fine by her, but since he was coming here any minute she wasn't going to open the door to him looking demure and dumb, the perfect secretary and human wallpaper. No, she wanted to make him sit up and notice her! Today, she wasn't going to be wearing clothes—she was going to be making a statement. And she wanted Nick to get it, loud and clear.

She flicked through her wardrobe despairingly, then suddenly saw just what she was looking for—she had bought it while James was alive, to wear at a fancy dress party with a 1920s theme. James had loved her in it, but she had never worn it again because it screamed sex appeal, and made men stare so hard. It was a simple black sheath; the neckline just skimmed the curve of her breasts, the fringed skirt ended above the knee, leaving her long, slender legs bare.

Would it still fit her? she wondered, slipping into it. She was surprised to find it did; fitted perfectly. She brushed her russet hair, wound it up into a chignon, pinned with a black bow, painted her mouth a clear bright red, dusted her lids with gold and green so that they sparkled like the sun on summer water, and then stood back to stare at her reflection.

No! She couldn't let Nick Caspian see her looking like this—or Sir George, either. She could just imagine the old man's horrified face! She would have to change into something more suitable.

A second later the doorbell rang loudly. Her nerves jangled. Surely it wasn't him already? While she was wondering what to do, the bell rang again, even louder, and she hurried towards the stairs.

She expected it to be Nick, and yet when she opened the door and saw him she felt a strange little stab of fierce emotion, she wasn't sure whether it was shock or pain.

'You're early!' she said huskily.

Nick didn't answer. He was too busy staring, from the smooth white shoulders, the curve of white breasts, down over the clinging black silk to the long legs in their sheer black silk stockings.

Hot pulses beat at her throat and wrists, but she managed to say, 'Sir George isn't here yet, but he should arrive soon.'

Trembling slightly, she stood back, and he walked past her, elegantly sombre in a black cashmere coat which was open, showing her the dark grey pinstripe suit he wore. Tense from head to foot, she closed the front door, very conscious of the fact that he was watching her like a hawk. But what was he thinking? She suspected it was just as well she didn't know.

He took off his coat and tossed it on to a chair in the panelled hall, then wandered along, studying the paintings which hung along the wall.

'Perhaps you would like to wait in here?' Gina suggested, and he walked into the spacious green and gold sitting-room, glancing around at the décor, the gold velvet curtains, the eighteenth-century English porcelain in a glass-walled cabinet, the lovely art nouveau bronze of a dancing nymph which stood in a niche at one end of the room, before his restless eyes moved back to Gina again.

'Please sit down,' she hurriedly said. 'Can I get you a drink? Tea, coffee, or something stronger?'

He gave her a dry smile, his eyes ironic. 'You wouldn't be trying to get me drunk so that you can seduce me and persuade me to agree to anything Sir George suggests, would you?'

'Don't be ridiculous!' she burst out, her face burning.

'Is it? In that dress, you could probably talk me into anything!'

'I didn't put it on for your benefit!' she impulsively snapped, and his eyes narrowed, sharp and very bright.

'No? Then who's the lucky man?'

'That's my business!' Gina said, her green eyes spitting fire.

He stared at her fixedly, and she asked again what he would like to drink. For a moment he didn't answer, his face hard. Then he drawled, 'Well, I shall need a clear head for this discussion, so as I drank rather too much wine with my lunch I had better have some black coffee.'

'I'll get it for you,' she said, with relief at this chance to escape from the room and his company. 'Excuse me...'

In the kitchen, she began to percolate the coffee, her mind hyperactive. Why on earth had she lied to him, let him think there was some man in her life? She had done it to make sure Nick didn't think she had put on this dress for him—but lying was always a mistake. She wished she hadn't done it.

She got down cups and saucers, a cream jug, a sugar bowl, turned off the percolated coffee, and then looked around for a tray, only to discover that the housekeeper kept the trays stacked on the top shelf of the old Victorian dresser which rose to the very ceiling.

She climbed on to a tall stool, but still had to stretch on tiptoe to reach them, and that made the stool wobble.

'Be careful!' Nick's deep voice said behind her at that second. Startled, she slipped, gave a cry of alarm, and fell. Nick caught her before she hit the ground and held her firmly. At the same moment, the heavy silver tray crashed on the tiles with a sound like thunder.

The noise made her jump; startled, her green eyes flicked up to stare at him as his arms tightened around her. For a seemingly endless moment they stared into each other's eyes. She could hear her heart beating under her ribs, heavy and fast; and somewhere an echo of it— or was that his heart beating?

And then his head came down in an inexorable movement and his mouth closed over hers. She groaned, her eyes closing. She had been waiting for him to kiss her ever since they met; she had been lying awake at night wondering what it would feel like to be in his arms, and at last she knew.

His lips moved with such sensuality, warm and coaxing against her mouth; she kissed him back hungrily, pierced by an excitement like the stab of a knife. The long years when she'd slept alone, when no man's hand had caressed her, had created a need which rose clamouring now, pulsing deep inside her body like an open wound.

She put her arms around his neck, her hands grasped his hair, her body twisting and winding closer and closer to his while they kissed. He unzipped her dress, began stroking her naked back, one hand lightly brushing a path along her spine, the other hand sliding under her heavy weight of hair, caressing her warm nape with an intimacy which sent shudders of pleasure through her. His mouth softly moved down her neck and she groaned, trembling, desire drowning her ability to think.

Then from outside came the sound of a door slamming, followed by a key turning in the front door, then the grate of a voice in the hall.

Nick let go of her at once, and, hurriedly opening her eyes, Gina gave him a stricken look.

'That must be Sir George!' she whispered, her legs so weak that she had to stagger forward into a chair.

He nodded, a dark colour in his face, ran a hand over his tousled hair, to smooth it down.

'I'll go and talk to him. You deal with the coffee,' he said in a rough, almost harsh voice, turned on his heel and was gone.

Gina couldn't move for an instant. How could he pull himself together so quickly, after what had just happened? He had been flushed, and not altogether steady on his feet, but he had thought and moved fast enough. If she hadn't known what had been happening a moment ago, she would never have guessed, from Nick's face or manner. The passion which had flared between them hadn't meant much to him, had it? Or how could he have recovered so quickly?

Bitterness tightened her face. No doubt he had had plenty of experience in this game. How many other women had melted into his arms, lost to everything but those seductive hands, that sensuous mouth? Shame and guilt made her face burn. She gritted her teeth, despising herself. She zipped up her dress again, ran cold water over a towel, pressed the wet towel against her eyes and forehead. Her head was thudding with pain. She had to pull herself together. She couldn't face him again yet. She couldn't join him and the old man, sit in that room with Nick so close, feel his mocking eyes on her, the taunt of his amusement because she had given way to him so utterly.

Oh, but he had been so convincing. She remembered the deep groan of passion he had given, remembered the thick breathing, the heat of his skin, the shake in his hands as he caressed her.

He had completely fooled her. What an actor he was! And she had fallen for his act; hook, line and sinker. She screwed her hands up and felt like pounding them into her own face, but why should she hit herself—why not him?

The telephone on the wall behind her began to ring, the internal note which meant it came from one of the other rooms in the house. Startled, she stumbled to pick it up.

'Gina?' The old man sounded terse, irritable. 'Where's that coffee? I'll have some, too—forget the tea.'

'It's coming now,' she huskily said, and hung up. She stood there for another moment, breathing deeply, fighting for self-control. She must not let Nick see what he had done to her.

As she carried the tray through the hall, she paused to check her appearance in the mirror. Apart from ruffled hair, she looked shockingly normal, as though nothing had happened. She ran her hands over her hair, pushed stray tendrils back into the chignon, and looked much neater.

When she walked into the room, Nick was sitting in an armchair. He got to his feet as she entered and in a stride reached her, took the tray from her and placed it on a low coffee-table.

'You asked for black coffee, didn't you?' she said, not quite meeting his cool grey eyes, and was relieved to see that her hands had stopped shaking.

Nick took the cup she offered him, going back to his chair, and she took the old man his coffee. Sir George was staring at her fixedly, his grizzled brows lifted and a look of astonishment in his eyes.

'I haven't seen that dress before!'

She blushed, aware of Nick listening and watching. 'I've had it for years but I don't wear it often.'

'Hmm...' said Sir George, his tone implying that he wasn't surprised to hear it. Then he asked, 'Are you going out somewhere special later?'

She lied again, because she didn't want Nick to know that she had put the dress on for him. 'I might be.'

'Hmm,' said Sir George again.

'Shall we get on with our discussion?' Nick broke in tersely. The old man gave him a bitter glance, then looked up at Gina.

'Mr Caspian has just told me that he has bought Laura Dailey's shares.'

She bit her lip, then said, 'The first rat to leave the sinking ship?' and the old man nodded, giving a short sigh.

'Sir George, save yourself a great deal of trouble,' Nick Caspian said quietly. 'Admit defeat.'

The old man looked at Gina, his face helpless and hopeless. They stared at each other, neither speaking, neither knowing what to say.

'What choice do I have?' he asked rhetorically.

'None, I'm afraid,' Nick said. 'It's only a matter of time before you are forced into bankruptcy, unless you agree to my terms.'

Gina watched him bitterly. This was the real Nick Caspian, cold and ruthless, not to be trusted. Only a fool would fall in love with a man like this.

'You need a big injection of new capital into the company if it is to survive,' he calmly told the old man. 'And nobody lends that sort of money without some measure of control. You know that as well as I do.'

'Yes, I know that,' Sir George said in a tired voice. 'Very well. I admit defeat.'

Ice trickled down Gina's spine. He had won. Well, hadn't she known he would, right from the beginning? He was cruel, remorseless; a predatory animal in the jungle world of high finance and big business. He stalked his prey with endless patience, and he always made his kill. The old man had never been a match for him— when he was young he might have been, but now he was too old and tired. While he lived, the old man might retain the title of chairman, but from now on Nick Caspian was going to be the real power behind the *Sentinel*.

CHAPTER FIVE

TEN days later, Hazel was eating a peach yoghurt at her desk when the door opened suddenly, making her jump almost guiltily as she swung round to see who had appeared. She hated to be caught eating in the office, although she often brought a packed lunch to work if she knew she was going to have a busy day. It meant she could be sure of at least one quiet hour in which to catch up with any paperwork which had fallen behind, and Hazel hated to fall behind with any of her work. When Sir George had appointed her as his senior secretary she had leapfrogged over several older women, whose resentment was openly expressed, if in an oblique fashion.

'You're much too young,' they told her. 'You won't be able to do the work.'

And, when, after straining every nerve, she managed to prove them wrong, they said with pretended sympathy but through gritted teeth, 'It will be too much for you; you'll never keep it up, dear.'

They watched her like hawks, waiting for her to fail, or to show signs of weakness, but Hazel was determined to keep her job and do it supremely well, so she got into the habit of arriving early and leaving late, and skipping lunch whenever she felt the volume of work was growing too heavy. She tried not to be seen snacking at her desk, however, by any of the other staff, or even Sir George. Hazel preferred the appearance of effortless efficiency.

Today, though, it was not one of the other secretaries who interrupted her. It was Piet van Leyden, the wintry sunlight gleaming on his smooth blond hair and tanned skin. Hazel was just as horrified as if it had been one of her colleagues. She put down her tub of yoghurt and stood up, hoping he hadn't seen it.

'Sir George isn't here, I'm afraid, Mr van Leyden,' she coldly said. 'He will not be back for several hours. Can I give him a message?'

'I am not here to see Sir George, I was looking for Mrs Tyrrell, actually.'

'She is at lunch too,' Hazel informed him curtly.

'Do you think she will be back soon?'

'I have no idea.'

He gave her a sharp look, frowning. 'You are not being very helpful.'

Hazel stared back expressionlessly. 'Aren't I? Maybe that is because I am very busy, and I am not paid to keep track of Mrs Tyrrell's movements.'

'You are not very polite, either,' Piet complained, and this time she didn't reply at all.

She couldn't deny it. Nor did she want to. It was true; she was not being polite, or friendly, or helpful, but then she did not feel any of those things, confronted with Piet van Leyden. He spoke politely enough to her, but she was pretty certain he couldn't remember her name, wasn't quite sure who she was, and didn't care, anyway. A lot of the men who came to this office to see Sir George treated her with polite indifference or arrogance, and it didn't bother her—but for some reason it infuriated her to meet the same treatment from this Dutchman.

Her chin lifted and her eyes held his, steadily, until Piet looked away, his brows together.

He didn't leave, though. He wandered over to the window and looked out, one hand in his jacket pocket, jingling some coins audibly, then, after a moment, half turned to look at her again.

'I'm not surprised you're bad-tempered. This view is grim enough to depress anyone.'

'It's a typical London view, and I'm rather fond of it!' Hazel said, repressively, 'And I'm not bad-tempered! Just busy.'

He looked at her desk, saw the yoghurt, and grinned. 'And eating such a skimpy lunch won't cheer you up, either!' He flicked a glance down over her, his face amused. 'You certainly don't need to diet.'

'Mr van Leyden, if you have a message for Mrs Tyrrell, I will see she gets it!' Hazel bit out, and he gave her a wry smile.

'Thank you, Miss...?' His voice died away. 'Sorry, I've forgotten your name,' he admitted.

She had known he had, but she was furious. 'Forbes,' she snapped.

'Hazel Forbes,' he said, remembering. 'I like that name...Hazel...a lovely, graceful tree. One does not see it in England as often these days, I think. It used to be grown in coppices, didn't it? The wood was used for many things—from basket-weaving to furniture.' He came over to her desk and stared fixedly, which made her flush deepen and her nerves prickle with a strange heat. Why was he looking at her like that? Grimly, she decided that he was probably thinking that the name didn't suit her! If he said something like that, she would hit him!

She certainly didn't expect what he did say. 'Your eyes are the wrong colour.'

'What?' she muttered, taken aback.

'They should be hazel, to match your name—but they're no colour at all, really, are they?'

'Grey,' she snapped. 'My eyes are grey!'

He had already lost interest, turned away, looked at his watch. 'Will you ask Mrs Tyrrell to ring me, when she gets back?'

Then he was gone and Hazel sat slowly down behind her desk and looked at her half-eaten yoghurt with distaste. She didn't want it now. She looked out of the window at the London roof-tops and felt depressed, just as Piet van Leyden had prophesied.

He was only interested in Gina. He might have noticed her a little, but it was only to decide that her eyes had no colour at all and she was boring.

She threw her yoghurt away, wrote a curt note to Gina telling her he had called and wanted her to ring him, and then got on with her work, trying not to think about Piet van Leyden, or what was going on between him and Gina.

Gina was secretive. It was rare for her to mention her private life, and Hazel had no idea whether or not Gina was seeing anyone, let alone Piet van Leyden.

Once or twice, it had occurred to Hazel that Gina might be interested in Nick Caspian, but whenever she saw them together it was hostility that she felt flashing between them, not attraction, although it was often hard to tell the difference from the outside.

They were undoubtedly very aware of each other, though, for whatever reason. You couldn't fail to notice that if you were in their company for five minutes. Hazel could understand why Gina should be antagonistic towards Nick Caspian. He had snatched the *Sentinel* away from Sir George, and Gina loved the old man. It was not very likely that she would forgive anyone who had hurt him.

Hazel didn't see Gina read the note she had left her, and she was far too proud to ask her point-blank—are you seeing Piet van Leyden, or will you go out with him if he asks you? In the past, she had asked Gina such questions directly, cheerfully, and almost never got an answer, except one of Gina's shy smiles, a little shrug perhaps. Gina never talked about herself. And this time, somehow, Hazel couldn't bring herself to ask, anyway. She preferred not to know the answer to her question.

Piet came into the office again the following Monday, and this time Hazel was expecting him because he had an appointment with Sir George.

He had dressed for the occasion, too, she noticed immediately, her apparently cool eyes whisking over him from head to foot. He normally dressed very casually, if quite expensively. Today, though, he was in a lounge suit, well tailored, charcoal-grey with a very fine blue stripe in it, and his buttoned-down shirt too had a thin blue stripe on white. He had brushed his blond hair until it shone, smooth as glass.

'Good morning, Miss Forbes—I suppose I must not call you Hazel?' he said with a glint of teasing in his blue eyes, and she felt her body stiffen as if she had been given an electric shock by his quick smile.

She was almost unable to speak for a second, then managed to get out quite steadily, 'Good morning, Mr van Leyden. Sir George has someone with him at the moment. Please sit down; he shouldn't be very long. Would you care for some coffee while you wait?'

'Thank you, I should love some,' he said solemnly, but still with that twinkle in his eye that told her he found her funny.

She got up and went over to the table which held her coffee-making equipment, very conscious of the fact that Piet watched her every move.

She always dressed quite soberly for the office, realising it made her look older and more responsible. Today she was wearing a straight black skirt, a cream silk shirt, fine black stockings and black high heels. She was very slim; the outfit looked good on her, but she knew she was not as striking as Gina, whose fragility and vivid colouring were such an unusual combination, and she resented Piet's stare.

She handed him his cup without meeting his eyes or saying anything. Piet said, 'Thank you,' as she went back to her desk and she gave him a curt nod.

He sipped the coffee, raised his brows. 'This is very good, just how I like it—perfect.'

'Thank you,' she said without looking up, pretending to concentrate on her work.

He drank his coffee then got up to put the cup back on the table where she had made it, then, to her alarm, began to prowl around her office, opening cabinet drawers, looking at the precisely aligned rows of filed documents, came round and peered at her computer screen, at her immaculately kept desk.

Hazel was tensely aware of him standing so close to her, his body almost touching hers.

'You are a perfectionist,' he commented to her rigid profile.

Hazel didn't answer. Somehow she did not feel he intended the remark as a compliment.

'So neat, so elegant, so competent,' he said, and for once she could pick up a trace of his Dutch accent.

A pause, as if he waited for her to answer him, then he murmured drily, 'Terrifying.'

Hazel's teeth met and she was about to snap back at him when she heard Sir George's voice saying goodbye to the executive who had been in his office.

'I will see if Sir George is free now,' she said icily, getting up a little too fast, before Piet could get out of her way. They collided, Hazel began to fall, and Piet grabbed her to save her, his arm going round her waist.

She felt as if she had been punched in the stomach. For a second she couldn't breathe. They were face to face, their bodies warm against each other.

'You were in too much of a hurry to get rid of me!' Piet said, smiling crookedly, then he let go of her and stood back and she squeezed past him, very flushed, just as Sir George appeared in the doorway.

'Mr van Leyden,' he said courteously, extending his hand. 'I do apologise for keeping you waiting, I had an emergency meeting to deal with...come through...'

Piet followed him out of the room and Hazel sat down again, trembling faintly. She had never felt like this in her life before. The closest she had ever come to such sensations had been when she had flu once—she remembered being lightheaded, dizzy, shivery, hot and cold all at the same time, and that was how she felt now.

Well, I haven't got flu, she thought grimly. It must be love. She closed her eyes, groaning silently.

'What's the matter, Hazel?' asked Gina in a surprised voice, from the door. 'Aren't you well?'

Hazel hurriedly opened her eyes, very pink. 'I'm fine, I'm...just...I was thinking...'

Gina came over to sit on the edge of her desk, sur-
veying her thoughtfully. Hazel avoided her eyes. 'You're
tired,' Gina decided sympathetically. 'We all are. This
is a very difficult time, for all of us—I know I'm very
tense, myself. I shall be very glad when we finally make
this move to Barbary Wharf.'

'So shall I!' Hazel said with feeling. Once they had
moved to the new complex, she would probably never
see Piet van Leyden again, and she could stop feeling
like this.

A few weeks later, on her way back from lunch, Gina
visited the news department in search of Roz. The open-
plan floor was badly lit, windows were too high and there
were draughts blowing a gale through the room on winter
nights.

A telex machine chattered at each end of the room,
television blared in one corner, a radio in another, tele-
phones rang, computers and typewriters buzzed and
clattered, reporters shouted at each other above the din—
the noise was deafening, and yet now that they were
going to move to modern premises the reporters, who
had complained for years about the place, were all mel-
ancholy over the thought of leaving it.

'Where's Roz?' she asked a reporter at one of the
shabby old desks, raising her voice to be heard above
the clatter of the telex machine. He looked up, a ciga-
rette in one hand, a yellow copy slip he was reading in
the other, and grinned, gesturing towards a glass-walled
little box of an office nearby.

'Try the fish tank.'

Gina saw Roz then, standing in the enclosed office in
front of a cluttered desk behind which Daniel Bruneille

sat in his shirt-sleeves, his tie off, his collar open, his curly hair dishevelled, and his thin face aggressive.

She couldn't hear a word either of them said, because the glass used to construct the office was soundproof, yet it was patently obvious that they were shouting at each other, and she stared, fascinated.

'It's like a silent film,' she thought aloud.

The reporter laughed. 'Like two angry goldfish, you mean, opening and closing their mouths at each other. Why do you think we call it the fish tank?'

Gina didn't like to interrupt what looked like the latest battle in a world war; she turned to go, but just then Roz came out, slamming the door behind her, making the glass walls shiver and vibrate. All over the long office people looked up, grinning. Nobody seemed surprised. Gina got the feeling these rows erupted all the time. Daniel Bruneille sat at his desk glaring after Roz, visibly, but silently, swearing.

Hurrying to meet Roz, she eyed her warily. Roz looked as if she wanted to bite somebody.

'Hi, Roz, I heard you were back from East Berlin,' Gina said. 'Happy birthday.' She handed Roz a gaily wrapped package.

Surprise struggled with temper in Roz's flushed face. 'Oh! Thanks! How do you always remember?'

She tore open the package, while Gina watched. She had spent a long time looking for something she thought Roz might like.

She sighed with relief when Roz's face lit up. 'It's gorgeous! Wherever did you find it?'

'An antique shop. It's sixty years old, although you'd never guess, would you?'

'I hope you haven't been extravagant!' Roz flung the silk shawl around her shoulders with a graceful gesture; crimson poppies and golden ears of wheat were splashed across a black background. Gina had thought as soon as she saw it that the shawl had exactly the dramatic impact Roz liked her clothes to have, but you could never predict precisely how Roz would react.

'Glad you like it,' she said, and Roz turned to look at her, smiling.

'I love it!'

'It suits you! Have you got anything planned for to-night? Could we have dinner, and talk?'

Roz gave her a shrewd look. 'Problems?'

Gina nodded, unwilling to mention them with so many people around, and Roz suggested, 'Why don't we eat in at my place? I'll pick up a Chinese from a take-away on the way home.'

'Great.'

A deep voice with a strong French accent snarled, 'Where do you two women think you are? This isn't a catwalk or a beauty parlour. It's a newsroom! OK, Roz? If you don't want to work, so... get out and let the rest of us concentrate!'

Angry colour swept up Roz's face again and she spun on one foot to bite back at him. 'Will you stop hassling me?'

Gina quickly said, 'I was just going; sorry if I disturbed you, Mr Bruneille.'

'You didn't,' Roz told her, eyeing Daniel Bruneille with icy dislike. 'He couldn't hear a thing inside his fish-tank, he had to come out to eavesdrop—and now he's just grabbing the chance to needle me.'

'Hey! I run this office, you know!'

'We all know that, Monsieur Bruneille!' Roz sneered.

'*Bien*, Mademoiselle Amery!' he snapped back, his black eyes glittering, then slid back into his excellent, if accented English. 'And I still need your copy on my desk before the deadline tonight.'

'You'll get it!'

'I'd better!' he threatened, turning away, then paused, swept an assessing eye over her slender figure draped in the brilliant colours of the shawl, and said coolly, 'By the way, the shawl's spectacular!'

Roz gave him a startled glance, her lashes flicking down. 'Oh...thanks...'

'Almost makes you look like a woman!' Daniel said loudly, as he walked away, and all the other men roared with laughter. Roz's hands screwed up into fists.

'You see what I have to put up with?' she muttered, glaring after him. 'He never misses a chance to stick a knife in my back!'

Gina was glad to get away from the noise and clatter, and the tense atmosphere of the place. She knew she would never have made a reporter, either on the home desk or the foreign one.

There was too much competition, too much stress; Gina was not the type to cope with either. She was a gentle, quiet girl who preferred a tranquil life. She often wished she and James had had a baby. They had talked about it, but there had seemed to be plenty of time.

That evening Gina curled up on a couch at Roz's flat, after dinner, watching the evening news on TV with the sound turned off, waiting for an interview with Nick Caspian and Sir George which had been recorded that morning at the *Sentinel* offices.

A great deal had happened since Sir George had wearily accepted that he must accept Nick Caspian as a force in the company. Every day, the two of them, each flanked by lawyers and accountants, had had lengthy discussions about the future, although, to her relief, Gina had not been present, so she had no idea what they had talked about.

Only when the formal announcement was made did she discover that Sir George had sold Nick a parcel of the shares he had held. This transfer of shares didn't give Nick a controlling interest; Sir George retained sufficient shares to ensure that he and Nick each held the same number, but the city had been left in no doubt that the *Sentinel* was now going to be run by Caspian International, and the company shares had climbed even higher.

At the same time the new management had had interviews with the various staff unions, all clamouring for information, wanting assurances, promises that their particular members would not suffer in the upheavals which were obviously about to begin.

Nick Caspian had frankly told them that there were going to be redundancies in most departments, but he hadn't had time to decide where cuts were to be made, which had sent the unions into a furious tizzy. They wouldn't accept widespread redundancy easily, as Gina said to Roz.

'There is bound to be a strike,' Roz agreed. 'The question is...when? And which unions? I don't suppose Nick Caspian was very frank about that when he was interviewed, though—did you watch the filming?'

'From a corner—the lights were so hot my mascara ran!'

'And how did Nick Caspian perform under the lights?' Roz drily enquired.

'Cool as ice!' Gina sounded bitter, and Roz stared at her.

'You really don't like him, do you?'

'I don't trust him,' Gina evaded.

'I can see why!' Roz agreed. 'But, all the same, most women start having fantasies if you just mention his name! Come on, you have to admit he's sexy, even if he isn't the easiest guy in the world to like.'

'Well, if we're going to talk about sexy guys who aren't easy to get on with, what about Daniel Bruneille?' Gina asked tartly.

Roz flushed. 'What?'

'Sorry, that was a bitchy thing to say!' Gina hurriedly said, wishing she hadn't been so rash as to open her mouth.

Roz glared, then laughed shortly. 'No, it wasn't! If I expect you to face facts, I suppose I ought to face them, too. Daniel is a very sexy guy!'

Gina grinned at her. 'He is, isn't he? It's that French accent!'

'Does turn you on, doesn't it?' said Roz.

'He has wicked eyes, too,' said Gina.

'Bedroom eyes,' Roz agreed, sighing.

'And such long, long legs!'

'Hey!' said Roz, eyeing her with sudden suspicion. 'You don't fancy him yourself, do you?'

Gina gave her a teasing look. 'Well...' Then she laughed. 'No, gorgeous though he is, I know I could never handle him. He scares me a little bit.'

'He should do!' Roz grimly said. 'Daniel Bruneille is one of the most difficult guys it has been my misfortune to meet! And I've met quite a few! Today, for example, I'd hardly got off the plane than he was asking where my article was! I said, "Give me a chance to recover from a very hairy trip around what used to be East Germany," and he snapped, "Why? Just because you're a woman?" And this was right in the office, with everyone listening—of course, the other guys all laughed like crazy, and, although I was shattered by the trip and would have liked to put off doing my story until tomorrow, I had no option but to sit down and write it as fast as my fingers would move. Now I feel as if I'd suffered brain death.'

'You look half dead,' agreed Gina. 'Sorry, I shouldn't have teased you about Daniel.'

'No,' insisted Roz, 'I seem to have lost my sense of humour where he's concerned.'

'I know how you feel,' Gina said, 'I dread the sight of Nick Caspian walking into the office.'

It was true, but what she did not tell Roz was that if a day went by without her seeing him she was restless and irritable for no reason, and when he *was* there she felt as if every one of her nerve-ends had been charged with electricity. Nick had been busy all week with this take-over. The only times they had met had been when she was accompanying Sir George to some meeting.

Roz gave her a wry smile. 'Well, you are going to have to get used to that! He is going to be in the office a lot of the time.'

'But Sir George will still be chairman...'

'I doubt if that will be for much longer!' Roz commented cynically.

Gina winced. 'Don't say that!'

'Sorry,' Roz said, giving her a sympathetic look. 'But I know how Nick Caspian operates. He'll keep Sir George on the board as a figurehead, for just as long as it suits him, but Sir George's days as chairman are doomed.'

Gina paled. 'You're probably right, but... oh, if he pushes the old man out I'll... I'll...'

Roz gave her a wry, friendly smile. 'Kill him? You'd have to join the queue. A lot of other people have sworn to get Nick Caspian, but he seems to bear a charmed life. He is pretty amazing, you know. Caspian International has spread all over Europe during the last decade. He grows faster than moss.'

'I wonder how many newspapers he actually owns?'

'No idea now. But there's one good thing—he isn't likely to stay in London long. He'll soon be off elsewhere. He moves around a lot, keeping in touch with his various national companies, although he spends more time in Luxembourg than anywhere else.'

'Why Luxembourg?'

Roz gave her a surprised look. 'That's where the parent company is based.'

'I see. You know a lot about him, Roz!'

'I worked for him; it seemed a good idea to find out what I could. Information is always valuable.'

'What was it like? Working for him?'

Roz pulled a face. 'Well, I didn't exactly work directly for him, of course. Or with him. He just happened to own the paper I was working for!'

'But didn't your father work for him once?'

Roz looked surprised, staring at her. 'Yes, he did. How did you know that?'

'He told me he knew your father. He seems to admire him very much.'

Roz smiled crookedly. 'I believe he does! Odd, really. Dad hates men of Nick Caspian's type.'

'It's starting!' broke out Gina, turning up the sound, and they both sat forward to watch the interview. Nick was very impressive on TV; his grey eyes gazing directly out at them, his smile pleasant, his answers fluent. Sir George was gruff and flushed, gave brief answers, uneasy in front of a camera, and Gina's heart ached for him. He was hating the whole thing, and it showed.

The slim, blonde interviewer asked Nick, 'How soon will you be moving into the new Barbary Wharf site?'

'We hope to do so in a matter of months,' Nick coolly replied. 'The building is almost complete.'

'Are there likely to be redundancies among the staff?'

'Too far ahead to discuss the matter,' said Nick, giving the girl a limpidly charming smile.

The interview finished a moment later, and Roz switched off the set, giving Gina a wry look. 'That was what they call an evasive answer.'

'Of course it was!' Gina crossly muttered. 'He knows that a lot of staff will be shed, and he knows that that means a strike!'

In the office next morning Hazel said flatly, 'Watching that TV interview last night, I realised just how many changes we're going to have to face when Mr Caspian takes over. I think I ought to start looking for another job.'

Gina gave her a startled look. 'But your job isn't threatened!'

'As long as Sir George is working here, maybe not,' Hazel said quietly. 'But how long will that be? I think I'd rather go than be made redundant.'

'I think you would be wiser to wait,' Gina advised soberly. 'If you are made redundant they'll have to make you some sort of redundancy payment based on your years with the company. You don't want to lose that, do you?'

'I suppose you're right,' Hazel sighed. She was restless lately, she didn't know why. She had loved her job until very recently; but increasingly now her nerves were on edge and she was even finding herself getting irritable with Gina.

Flushed, she turned and looked out of the window. It must be the atmosphere in the office these days.

She had no reason for feeling cross with Gina. Oh, once upon a time, in the beginning, she had not been too sure of Gina's intentions, had been afraid Gina might be her rival in the company, until she realised she was being stupid. Gina was a Tyrrell, by marriage, at least. She didn't need to compete. One day, she would be a major force in the company when she inherited the Tyrrell shares, and she certainly wouldn't continue to be a secretary, however high-powered. It was obvious Sir George was grooming her for a top executive position, but Hazel suspected that Gina was not even conscious of the fact.

Hazel had learnt to be very fond of Gina. Gina was a very unusual human being. She had loved her husband for his own sake, not his money. She loved the old man, she liked to take care of him, to be with him when he needed her. Hazel, watching her day by day, year by year, had grown to like and trust her more than anyone she had ever known, and it upset her to find herself con-

stantly on the edge of losing her temper with Gina,
snapping at Gina, almost disliking Gina.

Nervous strain, she thought. That's what it is. Nervous
strain.

CHAPTER SIX

'You look pale,' Sir George said to Gina at breakfast one morning, frowning at her across the table. 'Aren't you well?'

'I do have a headache,' she admitted huskily.

'You sound throaty,' Sir George said. 'Maybe you're getting a cold. You shouldn't have got up. Stay at home today, go back to bed.'

She protested faintly, although she was glad of an excuse not to go to work. She was seeing too much of Nick there, and it would be a relief to be able to avoid him without being too obvious about it.

'You've been working too hard—a rest will do you good,' insisted Sir George, and wouldn't let her say another word. As soon as he had gone to the office, Gina went back to bed and slept for most of the morning with her curtains closed.

When she woke up it was half-past eleven, and her headache had gone, so she took a leisurely shower, her eyes closed and a blissful look on her face as she stood under the warm jet of water, feeling her whole body relax. She gently towelled her wet hair, slid into her short white towelling robe and wandered into her bedroom barefoot to choose something to wear.

Downstairs the doorbell began to ring, but she ignored it at first, expecting the housekeeper to answer it. She flicked through her wardrobe, lazily indecisive. Jeans and a sweater? A wool dress? If she wasn't going to the office she could be as casual as she liked. She paused, frowning, realising that the doorbell was still jangling. Why hadn't Daphne answered that? Maybe she was out shopping?

She went to her window to look out, caught a glimpse of the Rolls outside—the old man must have been worried about her and driven home on his way to lunch with one of the bank directors!

If nobody opened the door, the old man would be even more worried, so Gina ran downstairs as she was, barefoot, in her damp robe, her wet hair hanging round her flushed face.

She pulled open the door with a smile ready, then froze, her mouth open. 'You!' Only then did she realise she had mistaken his Rolls-Royce for Sir George's, which was the same colour and age.

'Me!' Nick coldly mocked, walking past her before she could slam the door shut again.

'I didn't invite you in!' she said, very flushed as she clutched the lapels of her robe, wishing it weren't so short. It ended at her thighs, leaving most of her legs bare, and from the way Nick was staring it was obvious he guessed she was naked underneath.

'Close the door, the wind is bitter,' Nick merely drawled, and he was right—the winter wind was sweeping through the hall, making her shiver, so she crossly let the door go and it slammed with a noise that echoed through the house.

'Temper, temper,' Nick said, eyeing her through his lashes with amusement.

'Sir George would not like it if he knew you were here, and he might be back any minute,' Gina threatened.

Nick grinned at her. 'He won't be—I just saw him drive off to have lunch with some guys from the bank.'

She bit her lip. 'Oh...' Her nerve-ends were leaping like candle-flames in the wind. Sir George would not be arriving—what if Daphne didn't come back for hours, either? She would be stranded here, in this house, with Nick.

'He told me you had stayed in bed this morning because you felt ill,' Nick said. 'I came round to see how you were. You don't look ill...' His grey gaze explored her again and she swallowed, blushing.

'I'm much better now. I slept for ages,' she stammered, trying desperately to think of a way of either persuading him to leave, or getting upstairs to dress. She couldn't stand here much longer in the damply clinging robe which left so much of her exposed to Nick's wandering eyes.

'Hmm,' he murmured, his mouth twisting. 'You got over it fast!'

'It was only a headache, and...Sir George thought I might have a cold...he insisted that I should go back to bed.' Gina was trembling, and very disturbed by the atmosphere between them even now, in broad daylight.

Whatever Nick's reasons for pursuing her, there was no denying her own awareness of him, the pulse of sensuality beating in her veins. She might tell herself she hated and despised him, but, however logical and cool her mind might be, her body was possessed with other feelings.

She couldn't hold his eyes and turned away, looking down. She heard Nick breathing close to her, then he moved, lifting a hand to touch her cheek caressingly.

'You look very sexy in that thing. It's driving me crazy just looking at you!' he said huskily, and she felt her heart roll over and over like a seal tossed in a wild sea.

Almost terrified by the force of her own emotions she slapped his hand down. 'Don't touch me!' she muttered, and heard Nick's angry intake of breath.

'All I did was touch your cheek, for God's sake! It was hardly a violent assault! What is it with you? Are you as cold as stone, or is it the way you always treat your men? Is it all a strategy? Is that how you got James Tyrrell to marry you? Refused to let him lay a finger on you and drove him out of his mind with frustration until he was ready to do anything to get you?'

Her face drained of all colour, a livid white out of which her green eyes glittered angrily. 'James and I were in love!' she said with hurt contempt. 'Don't try to to make it sound ugly. My God! How low are you prepared to sink?'

His features tightened and his eyes went dark. He stared down at her for a moment, his jawline taut, and then he said roughly, 'I'm sorry, you're right, that was unforgivable.'

She was startled by the apology, knowing how rarely Nick Caspian ever apologised for anything he said or did. She couldn't hold his searching gaze, and looked down, her lashes brushing her cheek.

'Sometimes when you're in this mood, you frighten me,' she whispered. 'You're too...too sudden.'

He laughed huskily. 'It doesn't seem so very sudden to me. We've known each other now for weeks, but I don't feel I'm getting anywhere with you. I want to get to know you better.'

'If you really think I tricked James into marrying me, you don't know me at all!' she said and he frowned sharply.

'Forget I said that. It was a vile thing to say, and I don't blame you for being furious. I didn't believe it, I know you're not like that, but I was too angry to care what I said so long as I hurt you...'

'Why should you want to hurt me?' Gina said in bewilderment and he looked down into her green eyes, then looked away, his mouth twisting.

'If you don't know, I can't tell you. Look, I have to fly to Luxembourg next week. Why don't you come with me?'

'Come with you?' she repeated, startled, her breathing quickening again.

'It would be a good idea for you to visit the base of my operations—you would learn a lot about Caspian International on a trip over there, and I'm sure Sir George will approve.'

'Oh, a business trip...' she said, and Nick looked at her through half-lowered lashes, a teasing, intimate look which made her colour start to rise again.

'We could combine business with pleasure.'

At once, she felt the flare of temptation deep inside her body, a hot ache which tortured her, but she didn't trust him. How could she when he could accuse her of tricking James into marriage? He didn't know her, he was right, and no man who could suspect her of such motives ever would know her or understand her. She met his eyes, fighting to make her face a blank.

'No!' she said, in a cool, firm voice, and Nick's black brows drew together.

'Scared? Gina——'

'No, not scared,' she interrupted. 'I simply don't want to go with you.'

His eyes seethed with violence then, and she began making hurried excuses, afraid of more confrontation.

'At the moment, I'm reluctant to go away, leaving Sir George alone. He's an old man ...'

'Surely he can spare you for a few days?' Nick demanded.

'He needs me,' she said, then stopped because he had come dangerously close and suddenly her heart was beating so hard it was deafening her.

'*I* need you,' Nick said hoarsely, and she saw the need in his eyes, the leap of a desire so hot that she began to shake.

She swallowed and whispered, 'I'm sorry, but ... I can't ...' and moved away, backwards, keeping her eyes on him like a rabbit staring fixedly at an advancing fox, so terrified it could not even save itself.

'Why not?' he asked in a sharper voice, his face all lines, angular and jagged with temper. 'Is there someone else, is that it?'

'Yes, that's right!' she said, in desperation, and his eyes flashed.

'Who is he?'

'None of your business!'

'I'm making it my business!' Nick said, and then his head swooped, his mouth covering hers before she could evade it.

The first touch of his lips sent her up in flame; she was trembling violently, and her lips parted in answering desire and Nick groaned, breathing as if he was drowning, his hand tugging at the belt of her robe until it unknotted and the lapels fell open.

He slid his hand inside to find her warm, bare flesh, and Gina gave an anguished moan as he softly touched her breast. She couldn't bear it, his fingers were so gentle, so caressing, her pleasure was piercingly sweet, but she felt pain, too, because she knew he did not love her, that his desire was purely physical, a craving of the body, not the heart...

'Gina...' he muttered, his hand wandering down the curve of her hip to her thigh. She had to close her eyes because the light hurt them; she craved for darkness, to hide from Nick how she felt, this burning deep inside her, this feverish need. It was as if all the passion she had pent up over the five years since James died was erupting now, exploding inside her with the brilliance of some firework display, colour and light and sound combining to take the breath away.

Nick groaned incoherently, burying his face in her throat, his skin hot against her. 'I've been thinking about holding you like this for so long—it seems like years, not just weeks! If we don't make love soon I shall go crazy. Gina, you must come to Luxembourg with me.'

She was shaking, just thinking about it, imagining it. Wanting it.

Nick's lips moved shakily down between her open lapels to her breast. His words breathed out on her flesh. 'We'll have to stay in my penthouse in Luxembourg City for a few days—but you'll love it there, the view is breathtaking, down into the Alzette River valley. You can go dizzy just looking out of the window. While I'm working, you can shop, explore, have fun, and once my business is over we'll escape to my lodge in the forest— it's only thirty miles from the city but we can be quite

alone there for a couple of days. We'll stay in bed, or
curl up by the fire, get to know each other...make love...'

Her heart turned over; she longed to say she would
go, but what was he offering her, after all? A brief affair,
a few ecstatic hours, and then it would all be over.

No, she wasn't giving in—she would hate herself if
she did. How long would it be before she saw him with
Christa Nordstrom again, or someone else like her? Had
to bear the pain of jealousy, the sting of humiliation?

She put both hands against his shoulder and pushed
violently. Nick must have been off balance—he reeled
backwards, swearing under his breath, and she re-tied
her belt with trembling fingers.

'Leave me alone, Nick,' she said unsteadily. 'Whatever
you say, or do, the answer is still no! I don't want to
have an affair with you. Take someone else to
Luxembourg.'

It took Nick a moment or two to pull himself together;
he looked at her almost incredulously. Maybe she was
the first woman who had ever said no to him, and gone
on saying it, however intense the pressure Nick piled on?

'You can't keep the lid on for the rest of your life,
Gina,' he muttered raggedly, his skin darkly flushed.
'You're a passionate woman, but ever since your husband
died you've been pretending you aren't—telling yourself
you don't need love. Nobody can get away with that for
ever. You're human, like everyone else. It's obvious that
sooner or later, even if you hadn't met me, there would
have been an explosion that blew your cosy little world
to kingdom come. Face up to your own needs.'

'My needs?' she echoed with bitterness. 'Not yours,
of course!'

'Mine, too,' he said quickly. 'I want you, of course I do. Trust me, Gina. Come away with me; we can get to know one another away from all this hassle. Sir George, the *Sentinel*, the whole battle—that has nothing to do with us.'

He was so devious. With his grey eyes gazing into hers, she could almost believe him when he said his battle for the *Sentinel* had nothing to do with them. Except that she knew he wanted control of the shares she might one day inherit!

His voice lowered, husky and pleading. 'Come on, darling, admit you're human and you need love as much as everyone else does—let me give it to you.'

She wanted to go with him so much she was shaking, but she would not listen to his siren voice. He hadn't said he was in love, had he? He had probably never been in love in his life. He wouldn't recognise love if he fell right into it and drowned—and one day she bitterly hoped he would do just that.

When Nick used the word love he meant sex. Admit you need sex, he was saying; let me give it to you—and no doubt he was good at it, he had had enough experience with enough women, and she had only ever been to bed with one man, which, in Nick's book, made her a wide-eyed innocent.

Well, she would rather stay ignorant than learn what he had to teach: how to cheat and lie and sleep around as though sensuality was all that mattered in this world.

'I admit it,' she said. 'I know I'm human—I've never said I don't want love, but I don't want what you call love, Mr Caspian. I'm not prepared to settle for a furtive affair... or anything else... with you.'

Nick's brows dragged together, and he turned pale, his grey eyes brilliant with rage. 'You wanted me just now, I could feel it—don't lie to me!'

'I've admitted that I'm human,' she threw back at him, very flushed. 'I have the same needs as everyone else, I can't help an automatic response when a man touches me like that—but that doesn't mean anything. Any man could get the same response; it wasn't personal, just a Pavlovian reaction.'

Nick scowled. 'That's not true!' His voice was fierce, a snarl. 'Not personal? You don't think I believe that? Damn you——'

He broke off, stiffening, as they both heard sounds elsewhere in the house. A door banging, movements, several thuds as if something heavy had been dropped, a burst of loud music and voices. Gina realised at once what it meant—Daphne had returned; she must have walked to the nearest shops through an alley which lead from the rear of the house to the paved pedestrian precinct nearby. Now she was in the kitchen, putting her shopping away while she listened to the radio.

The tension inside her sagged, she gave a little sigh, and Nick turned sardonic eyes on her.

'Relieved, Gina? Now, I wonder why you should be so glad we aren't alone any more?'

Now that there was someone in earshot, she was able to gaze calmly back at him and speak in a level voice. 'I'm glad because I'm sick of having to fight you off every time we are alone. Just stay away from me in future, Mr Caspian.'

She heard his sharp intake of breath and met grey eyes that leapt with angry menace. He was a modern man wearing elegant, civilised clothes, but under that surface there was something dark and primitive, she thought, shivering.

She felt like running, but she stood her ground, facing him, head up, trembling.

'Haven't you learnt by now that I never give up on anything I want?' he said harshly. 'I just keep coming back until I win, and I will win, Gina, you can be sure of that. The more you say no, the more determined I shall be to have you.'

'Not as determined as I am that you won't!' Gina bit back, her green eyes alive with hostility. 'The answer will always be no, however many times you come back. Now, will you get out?' She turned and opened the front door, held it, defying him fiercely.

Nick gave her a long, hard stare, then he was gone, banging the front door behind him. Gina heard Daphne exclaim, heard her coming towards the hall, her footsteps echoing on the woodblock floor.

She couldn't face talking to her so she fled, back upstairs to her bedroom, silently locking the door behind her before she sank down on to the bed, shivering.

A few moments later, Daphne knocked on her door. 'Are you awake?'

'Yes,' Gina said huskily. 'I'm just getting dressed.'

'Were you downstairs just now? I thought I heard someone.'

'Yes, I was looking for something.' To change the subject, Gina quickly added, 'What's for lunch?'

'Whatever you feel like! Are you hungry, or would you like something light, like fish or an omelette?'

'A mushroom omelette, and a little salad, would be perfect.'

'Shall I start getting it ready now? Look, why not have it in bed? Sir George said you were not to get up today.'

'I'd rather get up, I'm fine now,' Gina said. 'I'll be dressed and downstairs in ten minutes, OK?'

Daphne bustled away and Gina dressed in white cotton trousers, slightly flared in the leg, and a navy blue knitted top. She made up carefully, then went downstairs, hearing the telephone ringing faintly in the distance. Daphne would answer it in the kitchen, so she didn't bother about it, just walked into the sitting-room and turned on the television for the lunchtime news. A second later, the telephone extension in the room began to ring. Gina turned to stare at it, biting her lip—what if it was Nick? But she couldn't ignore it, so she picked it up.

'Yes? Who is it, Daphne?' she warily asked.

'A Mr Leyden to speak to you, Mrs Tyrrell,' the housekeeper told her. 'Shall I put him through?'

'Yes, thank you,' Gina said, and heard the call being transferred. 'Hello, Piet,' she said.

'How are you, Gina? Sir George was at Barbary Wharf this morning, and told me you had a cold and were staying at home today. I hope it is not serious?'

'No, not at all. I was rather tired, so I spent the morning in bed, and now I'm fine. I suppose this whole take-over business has been a strain for me, as well as Sir George.'

'Yes, it must have been a strain, for both of you,' Piet said sympathetically, then laughed. 'I rather envy you! I wish I could take a day off, too. But no chance of that! Nick Caspian is a slave-driver. He wants Barbary Wharf finished and he is relying on me to keep the work moving, which is not too easy. The British workman can be difficult.'

She laughed. 'I love your Dutch understatement.'

Piet said softly, 'I am happy to hear there is something about me that you love!'

Surprised by that, she blushed, glad he could not see her.

'You promised to have dinner with me, remember?' Piet went on. 'Is it still OK, or don't you feel well enough?'

'I'm sorry, Piet. I don't think I should go out. Perhaps we could make it tomorrow?' She liked Piet; he was attractive to look at, charming, friendly, good fun. Not the type she could ever take seriously, but that was just as well. She did not want any more complications in her life. Nick Caspian was quite enough of a complication.

Piet took it amicably, as he seemed to take most things. 'Of course, and if you feel worse tomorrow give me a ring. Otherwise, I will pick you up at seven.'

Daphne served her lunch five minutes later. The omelette was perfect, the salad crisp and fresh, but Gina had very little appetite. She ate sparingly, staring out of the window at the steel-grey sky—it was the colour of Nick's eyes when he was angry. Oh, stop thinking about him! she crossly told herself. Think about something else.

But what? Piet? She tried to imagine him, and was appalled to realise that although she remembered that he had blond hair and blue eyes his actual features were a complete blank—she couldn't conjure up his face however hard she tried.

Sir George said that Piet was one of Nick's closest colleagues. Was theirs a purely working relationship, or were they friends outside work? Did he know, for instance, that Nick was making passes at her? But she couldn't imagine Nick confiding his private affairs to anyone.

Colour stung her face. Why had she used the word 'affair'? They weren't having an affair! Nick had made a few passes at her, and she had slapped him down. Nick was very unlikely to tell Piet about that—and Piet was very unlikely to tell Nick that he was dating her. They had had a couple of evenings together, had dinner, gone to see a film. It had been very friendly, light and relaxed, nothing serious. Piet had not even tried to kiss her, and she liked that in him. He was not the type to make casual passes. He was very different from Nick.

Of course, it was possible that Piet was dating her solely because he knew Nick liked her. Men did play ego games with each other, using business or women as pawns.

But she couldn't believe that of Piet. No, if Piet did know Nick was interested in her, she was sure he wouldn't trespass on what he would probably see as his boss's territory? She had gained the distinct impression that Piet was somewhat in awe of Nick Caspian.

An angry smile curved her mouth. Nick wouldn't like it when he did find out she was seeing Piet! Not that he would be jealous; she didn't fool herself about that. Oh, Nick wanted her, but not because he loved her; his was a simple physical desire.

Nick would be angry only if he thought Piet had got her into bed, because Nick wanted to be the one who seduced her. He wanted her because she was resisting him, not because he loved her. He liked the hunt, the kill. Winning soothed his ego. He wanted to add her scalp to all the others at his belt, the way he added new companies to his list—Nick Caspian, the all-conquering hero of his own legend! Well, she was not going to be one of his trophies, like Christa Nordstrom, or the others before her!

She would go out with Piet and enjoy herself, forget Nick Caspian ever existed—she was going to have to forget him for the rest of her life; better start now.

CHAPTER SEVEN

NICK left for Luxembourg the following weekend, and to Gina's relief she didn't see him alone again before he went. She couldn't avoid him altogether, of course; he saw Sir George most days and she was always with the old man, at his elbow, helping him in and out of chairs, putting folders and letters in front of him, keeping a watchful eye on his energy levels, ready to whisk him away if he showed signs of collapse.

Every time she and Nick were in the same room she felt his cold eyes watching her. She thought of them as cold; steely slits between black lashes, ice-floes, bright, lethal daggers. And then she would look up and fire would flash out from them and they weren't icy any more, they were furnaces of rage and desire, and she would blink and flinch, and wonder why nobody else seemed to see the hot metallic sparks which filled the air.

On the Friday he told Sir George brusquely, 'Well, I'm off to Luxembourg tonight, in my jet. If you want me, you have my number there. I'll go on to Berlin after the board meeting, to deal with a little problem we're having there, and then I'm due in Madrid, where the managing director is going into forced retirement.' He caught Sir George's wry glance and added curtly, 'No, I didn't fire him. He had a heart attack. He'll live, but has to take it easy, so he's going. Only fifty; it's a tragedy for him and us. Brilliant man. I have to choose his successor.'

'So when will you be back?' the old man asked, and Nick shrugged, his gaze sliding briefly to Gina.

'Not sure. I'll let you know.' He turned as if to leave, then paused and said over his shoulder coolly, 'It might be useful for Mrs Tyrrell to come to Luxembourg for this board meeting. She would get a clearer idea of the working of the international company.'

Sir George looked startled, gave her a quick, uncertain glance. 'I suppose that's true—it hadn't occurred to me. Do you want to do that, Gina?' He left the decision up to her. She sensed that Nick had hoped he might urge her to go, but if he had he was disappointed.

'Oh, what a pity, I'm sure I would have learned a lot,' she said sweetly, meeting the furious flare of Nick's eyes with triumph, knowing he picked up on the double meaning in her words. 'But,' she added, with a mock sigh, 'I'll have to take a rain-check, I'm afraid. I'm busy this week.'

'Very well,' he said through his teeth, and she hoped Sir George couldn't hear the barely suppressed rage in his voice. Turning away from her, he said to the old man in a clipped voice, 'I'll probably talk to you from Luxembourg every day, but if there's so much as a hint of union trouble you will let me know at once, won't you?'

'You're expecting it?' grunted Sir George and Nick grimaced.

'While the cat's away the mice will play.'

'I'm afraid you're not their favourite man,' the old man told him with grim amusement.

'I don't aim to be,' Nick retorted. 'Popularity isn't top of my list of aims for the year.'

'Just as well,' muttered Gina, tidying the sheaf of papers he and Sir George had been discussing.

'What was that?' Nick turned on her, teeth bared.

'Only a joke,' she said.

Nick remembered Sir George and forced a smile. 'Not a very funny one!'

'Sorry!' she said, her eyes lowered but all her senses aware of him, the drag of his breathing, the rustle as he picked up his own documents, the musky scent of his aftershave.

'I must get moving,' he told Sir George, swinging round to him again, and then she heard him walking away, the old man beside him.

She wouldn't see him for a week, maybe more. Her heart beat slowly, heavily. She didn't look up, though, pretending to be too busy even to notice his departure. She heard him saying goodbye to Sir George at the door, felt his backward look, then he was gone, without another word to her, and she felt as if part of herself had been amputated.

Day after day dragged by, the following week seemed endless to her, although she was kept very busy both at home and in the office.

The countdown to the move to Barbary Wharf had begun now. The shredding machines were hard at work, disposing of generations of paperwork in all departments. Spider-haunted cupboards were opened and emptied, filing-cabinets cleared, old furniture labelled for disposal since the new complex would have entirely new furniture.

Sir George several times toured the old building, leaning on Gina's arm, visiting each floor in turn, remembering the past and perhaps trying to impress images on his memory before they vanished. He talked all the time about 'the old days'; seeming almost to forget she had not been there, too.

In the accountant's department he stared at the young women sitting at their computers, and shook his head. 'When I started in here we had clerks in black coats and stiff collars, wearing green eyeshades to cut down eyestrain, sitting on high stools in front of leather-bound ledgers, writing in them in copper-plate handwriting, using pen and ink.'

'It sounds like a scene out of Dickens,' Gina said, glad she had not worked in an office then.

Sir George chuckled wheezily. 'It was, it was. There was quite an atmosphere, though. I thought it was romantic.' He looked around the bright, modern-looking room, lit by fluorescent strips in the ceiling, the walls painted cream, a carpet on the floor. 'You couldn't call this romantic!' he said in disgust.

'It's probably more comfortable to work in, though!' Gina gently suggested and he snorted.

'Well, let's go down to the printing works now.'

He leaned on her young strength as they made their way to the lift, and Gina's forehead wrinkled in anxiety. He was so frail; he was ageing daily, and that was Nick's fault. He had taken away Sir George's reason for living, his family inheritance, his lifetime's obsession, the *Sentinel*.

'Now, this place hasn't changed much,' Sir George said in the gloomy cellars of the printing works where the thunder of machinery could be deafening once the electrician pressed the button which started the presses on their nightly print-run.

Gina looked around, grimacing, but the old man was unaware of her, he was staring fixedly into a past which would never return.

'When I was still a schoolboy, long before I came to work on the paper, I remember the first time I saw the printers rush out for their break. They came up from the printing works, like a river of lemmings, making for the pub across the road, where the barmaids already had the pints of beer lined up on the counter, in great rows, all round the bar. The men would be glistening with sweat, red-faced and in their shirt sleeves, some of them just in their vests, or wearing aprons—and their throats would be as dry as ash. They could drink pint after pint without getting drunk, just replacing what they sweated down in the works. It's like an oven down here in summer and even in winter it can be very hot.'

Gina looked around at the dirty walls, the grimy ceiling, the machinery. She didn't see them with the eye of nostalgia, and made a face. 'I would hate to work down here. You'd think they would be thrilled to move to the new printing works, instead of threatening to go on strike over it. Think how much easier their lives will be, working in clean, well-lit, modern surroundings instead of this hellhole.'

'People like what they know,' Sir George said with bleak tolerance. 'I don't want to move to Barbary Wharf myself, any more. I thought I did, but I'm too old to change. The day we leave Fleet Street will be the end of my working life. I didn't plan it that way, but thanks to Caspian that's the way it will be. For me, and a lot of other people who have worked for the *Sentinel* all their lives.'

She brushed her cheek against his arm, close to tears. 'Don't be silly, you'll never stop work. You'll still be involved in the *Sentinel* after we've moved. You'll still be chairman.'

He laughed grimly. 'I wonder. I don't trust Nick Caspian. Since he put all that capital into the company and pulled us out of trouble, he has had the other members of the board eating out of his hand, ready to believe every word he says, but they don't know the real man.'

'Do you think you do?' she asked uncertainly, wishing she did. You couldn't compartmentalise a man—the Nick Caspian who ruled a vast newspaper empire was the same man who was pursuing her with such obsessive and ruthless determination and it would help to know what made him tick.

'I know one thing for certain,' Sir George said drily. 'Nobody could acquire an empire as big as that without being as ruthless as Attila the Hun. Caspian has gone through Europe like a knife through butter over the past decade. He inherited a newspaper chain from his father fifteen years ago, and he has more than quadrupled it. You don't do that in such a short time by being chivalrous or kind to animals. I doubt if anybody knows exactly what methods he used to get what he wanted, but everyone knows he is a very hard man to do business with! And, in spite of his assurances about my future on the board, I don't feel safe.'

Gina fell silent, her face pale, and they returned to the boardroom floor a few minutes later, so that Sir George could chair yet another meeting of the heads of staff. He didn't need Gina to attend it, so she went back to her own office where she found Hazel studying the chart on the wall which showed the various stages in which the entire newspaper would be moving to Barbary Wharf.

'I'm still a bit hazy about timing,' Hazel said ruefully, looking round at her. 'This chart is very pretty, with all the different colours we used to set out dates and times and departments, but I still have the sinking suspicion that in the week itself there is going to be one enormous muddle.'

'Stop worrying,' urged Gina. 'This time next year you'll have forgotten we were ever working anywhere else!'

The phone rang and Hazel automatically picked it up. 'Sir George Tyrrell's office,' she said, then curtly, 'Oh, it's you!'

Gina was surprised by the ice in her tone, and stared at her. Was it Nick, ringing from Madrid again? He had already rung that day. Was something wrong? Was he coming back unexpectedly? Her heart began to beat so fast that it made her dizzy.

'Yes, she's here,' Hazel was saying in that cold, clipped voice. She held the phone out to Gina. 'Sorry, I forgot this was your office,' she muttered. 'It's for you.'

'Who is it?' asked Gina, hanging back without taking the phone, in case it was Nick.

'Piet van Leyden,' Hazel said, pushing the receiver into her hand.

Turning on her heel, she walked out of the room, and Gina stared after her, grimacing. Hazel had the memory of an elephant, and, because he had snubbed her on their first meeting, didn't like Piet at all, which baffled him, poor man. He was used to being popular wherever he went, especially with the opposite sex.

'Hello, Piet,' Gina said into the phone.

'Why does that woman hate the very sound of my voice?' he plaintively asked her. 'I only have to say hello for her to snap at me like a hungry crocodile.'

'Oh, dear,' Gina said helplessly, laughing. How could she tell him that he had offended Hazel by not even noticing *her* because he was so busy staring at another woman? Especially as the other woman was herself!

'Or isn't it me?' asked Piet. 'Maybe she just doesn't like men?'

'Oh, she likes men,' Gina drily told him. 'And they like her.'

'Oh?' Piet said offhandedly, sounding as if he was already bored with the subject, but then asked, 'She's going out with someone?'

Gina laughed. 'Hazel has always had a good-looking man in tow. If you come to the big "Farewell to Fleet Street" party you'll probably see her latest one, whoever it is. I can't keep up with them all. She's always changing them.'

'Is she?' Piet said. 'I don't see her as a *femme fatale*. She's such an iceberg; efficiency itself, of course, but so remote. This I do not like.' He was sounding Dutch again, which usually meant that he was either cross or nervous, and Gina wondered which it was this time. 'But I am looking forward to the party,' he added, changing the subject. 'Is it true that you're taking over the whole of some hotel?'

'Yes, the Old City Hotel. The party is in the ballroom and a lot of people wanted to stay the night rather than go home early, or not risk drinking at all. So Sir George suggested we took over the whole hotel. They agreed because it's the dead season—Christmas and New Year are over, and spring seems a long way off. This is quite a big hotel, but a ramshackle old Edwardian place. Its great advantage is that it's close to Fleet Street and very convenient.'

'And I suppose you are all excited about the move now that it's about to happen?'

'Well, actually,' she said drily, 'I think people are beginning to panic because there's still so much to do. Hazel is snowed under with work, but she is very patient and good-tempered, she won't fall to pieces the way some people have.'

'Patient and good-tempered?' repeated Piet in a heavily sarcastic voice. 'Are we talking about the same woman?'

'You're just prejudiced!' Gina said, laughing and glancing over her shoulder guiltily, in case Hazel was in earshot. Hurriedly, she asked, 'Why did you ring me, Piet? Just for a chat? Because, nice though it is to talk to you, I'm supposed to be working, and there is a lot to do just now!'

'No, to ask you to a film première in Leicester Square tomorrow. I know one of the stars, Bianca Valence—I designed her a villa in Italy while I was on holiday one time, and we've more or less kept in touch since then. She has sent me two complimentary tickets for the première.'

'What's the name of the film?'

'*Prospect of Moonlight.*'

'Oh, yes, I've heard about that. I'd love to come,' she said, mentally going through her wardrobe. 'Do we wear evening dress?'

'Of course! The dressier the better on these occasions!' Piet told her and a moment later rang off.

Gina replaced the phone and got down to work again, and a few minutes later Hazel returned. Gina gave her a sideways look and a rueful smile.

'He's really charming, you know!'

'To you, maybe. Not to me,' Hazel coldly said, and Gina surveyed her with thoughtful eyes. The two of them seemed fated to be at odds with each other—maybe they just were not on the same wavelength?

'Can we get on with this job?' Hazel asked in a curt tone. 'I have a lot of other things to do.'

Gina sighed and dropped the subject. Some time later Hazel offhandedly asked her, 'What did he want, anyway? Where is he taking you this time? A play or dinner?'

'He knows Bianca Valence and she gave him free tickets for her latest film première—it sounds as if it will be a very glitzy occasion!'

Hazel shredded a whole pile of documents before she said anything else, then she muttered, 'Did he date her, as well as work for her? He gets around, doesn't he?'

'I think she was just a client!' protested Gina.

Hazel gave her a cynical, angry smile. 'Is that what he told you? Well, he would, wouldn't he? I'd take that with a pinch of salt if I were you. She's always in the gossip columns and she always seems to have a new man with her. She obviously likes men, and someone like Piet van Leyden is too good-looking to have had a purely professional relationship with her. She was bound to fancy him; he's a bit like a film star to look at, isn't he?'

Gina gave her a startled, thoughtful look. 'I didn't think you liked him?'

Flushing, Hazel snapped, 'I don't, but I'm not blind.'

'No,' Gina agreed, smiling.

'What's so funny?' Hazel demanded, very pink and with suspicious eyes, and Gina shook her head.

'Nothing, just——'

'Just what?'

'Nothing. Have we finished shredding now?'

Sometimes Gina couldn't help wondering—exactly how did Hazel feel about Piet?

She didn't need to ask herself that question. She knew she was never likely to fall in love with Piet, much as she liked him and enjoyed his company. For the moment, their relationship was fun, and without stress. Piet wasn't making any demands on her; he made it clear he found her attractive and liked her but he didn't try to force the pace or make any heavy passes.

Gina was enjoying having his company on trips around London at weekends, to see museums, or visit art galleries, or admire famous buildings. Piet loved to give her a tour of some church or old house, explaining how it had been built, by whom, and extolling the splendours of various periods of architecture. He was astonishingly knowledgeable, he really knew his trade, and she was stunned by his grasp of the whole history of European architecture.

He made her feel useless and stupid because she had never taken the time and trouble to follow any particular career or acquire that sort of knowledge of anything.

She said something of the sort to Hazel later that day. 'I'm beginning to think I should stop working here and start taking a course in journalism, or business management, or something. I used to have fun working for Sir George, but I was only playing at working, and since

the take-over I've realised I'm just an amateur in a professional world.'

'Is that what Piet van Leyden has been feeding you?'
demanded Hazel, bristling, her grey eyes angry. 'Take
no notice of him! OK, he knows all about architecture—
well, he should! That is his job. But you do know a lot
about newspapers. You aren't just an amateur, any more
than I am. I trained for my job; you've had your training
doing the work—but you're good at it. You deal with
people sympathetically, you're efficient and you run Sir
George's home, look after his diet, take care of him.
Come on, you have lots of skills! If he had to pay
someone to do all the things for him that you do, it would
cost him a fortune. He would need a nurse, a companion, a private assistant...'

Gina began to laugh.

'I mean it! It isn't funny,' Hazel said, looking furious.
'You shouldn't undervalue yourself like that, or let Piet
van Leyden do it, either.'

'He doesn't, but thanks for the confidence boost,'
Gina told her affectionately. 'I wouldn't walk out on the
old man, anyway. He needs me. I'm all he has got.'

'He's lucky to have you,' Hazel said stubbornly, then
she looked at the clock and gave a groan. 'It's nearly
five o'clock already, and we still have masses of work
to get through.'

'Sorry, my fault, talking instead of working!' said
Gina, pulling a face, and they both concentrated after
that. There was so little time left now before the big
move to Barbary Wharf, and so much to do, that they
were beginning to doubt they would ever finish before
the removal vans arrived.

Sir George called them both in to his office before Hazel left for home. Sitting behind his desk, his gnarled, bluish hands clasped in front of him, he asked how their preparations were going, and they both stalwartly assured him they would be finished soon, avoiding each other's eyes.

'Good,' he said, smiling. 'I've been thinking—you and Hazel ought to go down to Barbary Wharf together to familiarise yourselves with the layout of the new offices before you have to move in there. Tomorrow morning would be fine. I shall be out of the office and I won't need either of you. Take a taxi there and back.'

Next day when they came out into Fleet Street to get into their taxi, they found that the weather had turned wet and windy—a February day which was more like March—with a livid grey sky filled with scudding darker clouds.

The Barbary Wharf site was completed now, although workmen were still everywhere, putting the final touches to the décor, checking that nothing had been overlooked.

The taxi driver whistled as they drove up to the electronic gates now guarding the main entrance.

'Like a fortress, ain't it? How do you get in?'

'We have security passes,' Hazel informed him, opening her handbag and getting out the plastic wallet which contained her photograph and signed pass.

'I don't fancy driving in there—would you mind if I drop you here?' the taxi driver said with another uneasy look through the ironwork gates as the security man peered out at them from his glass-walled kiosk.

'In this rain?' Hazel said, but in a resigned tone. She and Gina climbed out of the taxi and paid the driver, then showed their passes to the angled TV camera through which the security man was observing them. A side-gate swung open silently, and they went through.

A high blank black wall surrounded the entire complex now. They had to cross a windswept pedestrian walkway to reach the office block. Rain beat down on them, whipped their hair around their faces, and they began to run to get inside as soon as possible, their coats flapping wetly around their ankles.

The main entrance had double glass doors, one of which was pushed open from inside before they reached it and to her surprise Gina saw Piet standing there waiting for them. His smooth blond hair gleamed, his blue eyes held a smile of welcome as he waved to them, and she gave him a friendly smile back.

Hazel didn't smile; she was scowling. 'Not him!' she muttered, putting her head down in the face of the driving wind and rain, so angry she didn't notice the obstacle in her path.

A workman had left a bucket of white paint near the door. 'Look out, please!' Piet shouted, too late. Hazel ran straight into it and tripped. The bucket fell over, and Hazel fell too, sprawling on the paved walkway, face down.

Gina stopped and turned, in time to see Hazel getting up. Her face dripped white paint. Her hair was a sodden bird's nest. Her neat pale blue raincoat was muddy and wet.

Unfortunately, Piet gave a roar of laughter. Hazel didn't. Looking down at herself, she began raging, tears in her eyes. 'Oh... look at me... Stop laughing, you, you... wait till I... Oh!' She stamped her feet like a child, her hands screwed into fists at her sides.

Gina tried not to laugh, feeling terrible because it was one of the funniest sights she had ever seen, but Hazel was not in any mood to see the joke. She rushed to help her, but Piet got there first.

He produced a clean handkerchief, and deftly began to wipe Hazel's paint-stained face.

'Leave me alone!' Hazel snapped, snatching the handkerchief away to finish the operation herself.

'Come in out of this rain!' said Piet, smilingly watching her scrubbing away at her white-striped nose.

'Oh, shut up!' Hazel raged, her brown hair plastered down over her forehead, rain dripping down her neck.

Piet gave her a wry look, put an arm around her waist before she had notice of his intention and lifted her off the ground.

'Put me down!' shrieked Hazel, but he ignored her, merely ran with her tucked under his arm as if she was a doll.

Hazel tried to get away from him, legs kicking, arms flailing, but Piet simply laughed at her struggles as he carried her out of the pelting rain and howling gale. Only when they were inside did he let Hazel's feet slip to the ground.

'You . . . you . . .' seethed Hazel inarticulately.

'Kind man?' Piet suggested, trying to look serious, but only too obviously doubled up with silent laughter.

'Stop laughing!'

'I am sorry,' Piet said. 'There is a cloakroom at the end of this corridor.'

Hazel glared. 'It isn't funny!'

'No,' he agreed, struggling with his facial muscles.

'One of your workmen left that bucket in a stupid, dangerous place, and it's lucky I didn't hurt myself!'

'Very lucky,' he said, opening those beautiful blue eyes very wide and looking sincere and concerned. 'You didn't, did you?'

'No,' she had to concede, with sulky reluctance, obviously wishing she could claim she had damaged herself beyond repair. Her voice rose. 'But I might have done!'

'Yes, you might,' Piet said, nodding. 'And I shall speak very sharply to whoever left that bucket there. Now, let me show you to the cloakroom.'

'I can find my own way!' Hazel said, squelching as she began to walk down the corridor in her rain-soaked shoes. Piet couldn't hold back a snort of laughter at the sound she made with each step, and Hazel turned on him, flushed and furious.

'Don't you laugh at me!'

'Sorry, sorry,' Piet said, holding up his hands as if to defend himself. 'I can't help it, you do look so funny, those streaks of white paint on your face make you look like a Red Indian, especially when your hair is slicked down like that, you look as if you've been scalped! And your coat is muddy and your tights...' He ran a lingering eye over her from head to toe, his face alight with laughter. 'I've never seen you look like this before... you're always so neat and tidy, the perfect secretary, not quite human...'

Hazel's mouth rounded with fury. 'Not quite human!' she echoed, her face a hot pink.

Piet looked down into her angry grey eyes and his face changed. 'Like this you are!' he said, sounding surprised. He stared harder, said slowly, 'Like this, you're funny and sweet, with that little curl right in the middle of your forehead, like the English nursery rhyme. You know? "There was a little girl, who had a little curl, right in the middle of her forehead, and when she was good she was very, very good, but when she was bad she was horrid''.'

He recited the words in a sing-song chant, smiling, and Hazel stared back at him, her lips parted on a gasp, and didn't seem to have anything to say; a new departure for her, because Hazel was never at a loss for words. Super-efficient, calm and capable, Hazel—lost for words?

Gina watched them closely. Hazel had always been so hostile to Piet, but she was looking at him so oddly, a shy, hesitant look, and she was blushing, distinctly blushing.

For weeks now, Gina had been trying to decide how Hazel really felt about Piet—and, come to that, how Piet really felt about Hazel, because they had both been very ambivalent about each other. Hazel had been hostile from the start, had spent the last few months muttering rude things about him and bristling every time she saw him, and Piet had begun by being blankly indifferent to her, and then had constantly talked about her to Gina, complaining about her attitudes, asking questions about her, being belligerent about her all at the same time.

Hazel wasn't so conceited that she expected every man who saw her to swoon at her feet, and Piet was usually ultra-polite and kind to everyone—could their mutual antagonism have had a deeper cause?

There was something of the same jagged, explosive mix in the way Gina felt about Nick Caspian. Perhaps relations between the sexes were always complicated and contradictory?

Piet was staring down at Hazel as if he had never seen her before, his face quite stunned. Well, that wasn't surprising because, as he had just said, Hazel had probably never in her life looked this way before—muddy and wet and totally at a loss.

The super-efficient, carefully dressed Hazel of the *Sentinel* office had vanished, and left in her place this bedraggled creature whose defences were definitely down, who was off balance, vulnerable, helpless.

Gina watched as Piet's blue eyes lit with a smile, moved by her, full of charm and gentleness. Gina had seen him look like that before, but Hazel hadn't. He had never showed her his private personality.

'You look lovely,' he softly said, and Hazel blushed even more.

Well! thought Gina. Life is funnier and more unpredictable than we ever imagine.

CHAPTER EIGHT

PIET insisted on escorting both girls around the complex, in which he now took a personal interest, since he had been responsible for it for quite a long time. He was obviously proud of the fact that he had succeeded in speeding up the rate of progress without too much trouble with the workmen, and looked pleased when Gina congratulated him on the astonishing speed at which the complex had finally been completed.

Hazel murmured something polite, too, but Gina noted that their eyes never met. Piet answered, offhandedly. She felt like banging their heads together, and would dearly have loved to say something to each of them, but knew it was wiser not to interfere.

That afternoon Gina was kept busy helping Sir George with arrangements for a celebration dinner which the *Sentinel* was giving to leading figures of the day—politicians, artists, sportsmen, members of the royal family, writers, architects, some of the landed gentry, and wealthy businessmen. The first list was enormous; it was hard to whittle it down but there was limited space at the tables in the Savoy, where the party was to be held two days before the *Sentinel* left Fleet Street for ever. The party at the Old City Hotel was on the preceding night, after which many of the staff would be taking time off while the removal took place.

Piet arrived to pick her up promptly at seven, for the film première. He was in formal dress, immaculate in

140

crisp white bow tie and black evening jacket, and Gina was wearing her jade-green silk Grecian-style dress, with matching jewellery; an emerald and diamond necklace, earrings, and bracelet which Sir George had given her when she married James. She rarely wore the set—they mostly reposed in the family safety deposit in the bank, and they would be going back there first thing tomorrow.

'Magnificent,' Piet breathed, staring. 'They're the real thing, aren't they?'

She wryly nodded. Gina always felt uneasy wearing them; partly because she had not grown up in a world where such valuable objects were casually worn, and partly from fear of losing them.

She never really felt they belonged to her; she was merely using them for the moment, almost as if she had borrowed them from their real owner.

'I shall be very nervous going out with you in those!' Piet said wryly.

'Shall I take them off?' she asked uncertainly, but he shook his head.

'No, we haven't time—we mustn't be late, whatever we do, or we won't be allowed into the cinema after the royal party has arrived.'

Leicester Square was clotted with staring, applauding crowds who peered to see if she and Piet were famous faces, and, when they had decided that they weren't, turned away to look for someone more interesting.

They pushed their way through the hordes of glossy people in the foyer, all trying desperately to be seen talking to even more famous people than themselves, and finally made it to their seats.

It was a good film, and Bianca Valence gave an astonishingly good performance. Piet's eyes shone as he glanced sideways at Gina as the lights went up again. 'She was superb, wasn't she?' he said proudly, as if he owned the star.

'Brilliant,' Gina agreed, smiling back and wondering if he had had a brief romance with the famous name. What had happened in Italy, apart from Piet designing a villa for the star? 'Thank you for bringing me, I really enjoyed it, Piet,' she said, then sat up, staring across the cinema. 'Oh, look! There's that TV star, Jack Quilliam— the one in the police series. Wait till I tell Hazel I saw him—she'll be green with envy.'

Piet grimaced, staring at the tall actor who was head and shoulders above everyone around him. 'What is so wonderful about him? He's an ugly guy who's going bald.'

Gina laughed. 'Hazel thinks he's sexy.'

'She's crazy,' Piet said shortly.

Gina gave him a sideways look, suppressing a smile.

Offhandedly, Piet asked, 'What about her boyfriend? Is he ugly and bald, too?'

Gina giggled. 'I don't know. You'll have to ask her.'

'And get my face slapped? Oh, no, I know better than to annoy Miss Forbes,' Piet said.

Everyone was on their feet, pushing their way out, so they waited for a while, but even so Gina got separated from Piet, carried away from his side by a tidal wave of people all trying to flow out of the main exits. While she was looking for him, she suddenly saw Nick and her heart stood still. Everything around her fell away—the faces, the noise, the glitter of chandeliers.

He couldn't be here, she thought stupidly. He wasn't due back yet. She must have conjured his image up because she wanted so desperately to see him.

Then the world came back: she could see again, hear again, and it was Nick, tall and devastating in evening clothes, moving away from her with his arm around another woman, guiding her protectively through the crowd.

Gina stared at them, transfixed. She recognised Christa Nordstrom even from the rear; the perfect silky sweep of the other woman's blonde hair, the slender figure, the way she carried her head.

Even in this audience composed largely of celebrities and wealthy people heads were turning to stare and people whispered her name. She was possibly one of the top three models of the moment, much in demand, the fragile bones of that hauntingly lovely face always on magazines.

Gina could tell that those were real pearls she was wearing round her throat—their milky glow was far too good to be fake—and that was a very expensive dress from a top London designer she was wearing. Hers was a glamorous lifestyle, and she was the perfect companion for a man like Nick Caspian on an occasion like this.

Gina's throat ached with tears she couldn't shed, here, in public, and she was relieved when Piet suddenly pushed through a knot of people to grab her arm.

'There you are! Hold on to me or you'll get lost again,' he said, and she grasped his hand and held it tightly while they fought their way outside into the cold night air. 'Wait here, and I'll go and look for our car,' Piet said. They had arrived in a chauffeur-driven limousine which had dropped them outside the cinema and should have returned to pick them up now.

He darted away and Gina stood back, out of the flow of the crowd moving away around the square, hoping Piet would not be too long.

She was freezing, even though she was wearing a warmly lined black velvet cape, and she was depressed. She wanted to get home. Two questions kept buzzing round and round inside her head, like angry bees—how long had Nick been back in London, and just how serious was his affair with Christa? They looked so intimate, so casual together, just now, smiling and leaning on each other as they walked. Were they in love?

She bit her lip, closing her eyes. Pain ached deep inside her; the pain of loving Nick and knowing he did not love her. She wished she could forget him, cut him out of her memory.

Piet came back, looking irritated. 'I cannot see the car anywhere, I am afraid,' he said, sounding more Dutch than usual because he was so angry. 'I will have to go and phone the limousine company. I am sorry, Gina. I will try to hurry.'

There was little chance of getting a taxi at the moment—there were too many other people in the square with the same idea—and Gina didn't fancy the idea of clambering on to a bus in full evening dress.

She was about to suggest that Piet should ring her home and ask Sir George's chauffeur to come and pick them up, when a voice said coldly behind Piet, 'Good evening.'

Gina went white, then red, staring into Nick's hard, grey eyes. Piet was even more startled, because he hadn't noticed Nick in the cinema and so had not been prepared to come face to face with him.

Swinging round, he grinned cheerfully. 'Nick! When did you get back? I thought you were staying for another week?'

'I changed my mind,' Nick said, staring past him at Gina. 'I decided there was something urgent I had to deal with.'

'Anything I should know about?' asked Piet, frowning.

'No,' Nick curtly told him.

'Problems?' persisted Piet.

Nick's mouth twisted. 'Nothing I can't handle.'

He was talking to Piet, but he was watching Gina, and she stared back, wondering what had happened to Christa Nordstrom? Had she gone home without him? Or was she waiting for him somewhere?

He was wearing an elegant black cashmere coat over his evening clothes now, and had a white silk evening scarf casually slung round his neck. He looked magnificent. She wanted to look away from him but she couldn't; she was mesmerised. He was standing some feet away from her, she didn't like or trust him, but she knew he only had to touch her and she could be lost.

'How are you two getting home?' Nick asked Piet, who explained about the hired limousine which hadn't turned up again.

'I was just going to ring them,' he added wryly.

'Never mind, I'll give you a lift,' said Nick.

Gina was horrified and opened her mouth to protest, then met the lethal glitter of his grey eyes and shut her mouth again. The last thing she wanted was to be driven home by Nick Caspian, but she saw that he was in no mood to allow her to argue, and, anyway, Piet would be with her so where was the problem?

'Would you?' Piet said, with a quick smile. 'That's great, I'm grateful, for Gina's sake most of all.' He tightened his arm around her, looking down at her. 'I am so embarrassed that she has to wait in the cold on a night like this!'

'It's not your fault,' she said.

'You are always so understanding,' said Piet. 'I shall ring the car firm and give them hell tomorrow, be sure!'

'My car's parked round the corner,' Nick said roughly and turned to stride off, leaving Piet and Gina to hurry to keep up with him.

'This is very lucky, running into Nick,' Piet said to her.

'I can't believe our luck,' she repeated with an irony lost on him but not on Nick, who gave her another of those bright, deadly glances.

He had a chauffeur this evening, seated at the wheel of the classic black Rolls which she had once mistaken for Sir George's. The uniformed man leapt out to open the door for them, and Nick turned to help Gina into the back of the limousine, his hand under her elbow, then climbed in after her and took the seat next to her, leaving Piet to sit opposite them.

'Your place is near here, isn't it, Piet? We'll drop you first,' he coolly said, and didn't wait for Piet to reply, just gave the order curtly to his chauffeur, who drove off.

Gina stiffened, sitting upright, her nerves jumping. She could not drive home alone in this car with Nick! She tried to think of some excuse for escaping but Piet was not happy either.

'Oh, I think I should see Gina home,' he said hurriedly. 'I took her to the cinema. You need not drive me back here afterwards, Nick, you can drop us both at Gina's place, and I'll take a taxi home later.'

'Don't be ridiculous,' Nick snapped. 'We're almost there and that sort of chivalry is out of date. Women don't expect to be treated as if they are made of glass, Piet. Not any more.'

'Is that why you didn't see Christa Nordstrom home?' Gina icily asked him and he gave her a quick, frowning look.

'You saw us in the cinema?'

She didn't answer his question, just said coldly, 'What did you do with her? Put her in a taxi or let her walk home?'

'Don't be absurd! She came with somebody else, and she went home with him.'

Piet said, 'I didn't see Christa. How is she? Has she got anywhere with her film ambitions, yet?'

'It looks very promising,' Nick said offhandedly.

The car slowed down at that moment, and drew up outside Piet's home. He sighed mutinously, but Nick's expression left him no chance to argue.

'I am sorry there was a mix-up over the limousine, Gina,' he said, leaning over to kiss her cheek lightly.

'It wasn't your fault, Piet,' she began, and then Nick flung open the door of the Rolls with a crash that made them both jump.

'Out you get, Piet!' he curtly said.

Piet grimaced. 'You are so impatient, Nick! I am going. Goodnight, Gina.'

He got out of the car and Nick pulled the door shut before Piet could say another word. The Rolls drove off and Gina looked back, waving. Piet was standing on the

pavement, staring after them, then they turned a corner
and he was out of sight.

Nick leaned back, his long legs stretched out in front
of him, his hands buried deep in the pockets of his
evening coat.

She didn't look at him directly, but she could see his
reflection in the window of the limousine and her heart
hurt inside her. Even if she never saw him again after
tonight she knew she would never forget the way he
looked, the black hair, the incisive profile, the strong
curve of the mouth, the determined jawline. Everything
about Nick was imprinted on her heart and mind.

The silence seemed to drag on and on, and with each
passing second she grew more nervous, afraid of being
alone with him. He glanced sideways at her, his brows
jagged black wings above those hard eyes.

'Was Piet the secret boyfriend you wouldn't tell me
about? I can see why you kept quiet, the pair of you. I
knew Piet fancied you, but it never entered my head you
might like him.'

'I can't think why!' she said crossly. 'He's charming,
and good-looking, and——'

'OK,' he bit out. 'OK, he's God's gift to the opposite
sex! All the same, I was stunned when Sir George told
me you were dating Piet, and while I was away I couldn't
get it out of my mind. I couldn't sleep or think about
business any more; I couldn't concentrate on anything
while I was away.'

She looked at him with silent contempt—he had been
afraid she might marry Piet and threaten his control of
the *Sentinel*, no doubt.

'Not even Christa Nordstrom?' she coldly asked after
a long pause, and he gave her a quick, sharp look.

'Jealous, Gina?' he murmured, and then his eyes took on a warm, teasing intimacy. 'You don't need to be. She and I stopped dating each other a long time ago—before I ever met you...'

'Then why were you with her tonight?'

'We're still friends,' he shrugged. 'But it isn't anything more serious now...'

'But you were lovers?' She asked the question deliberately—she needed to know, to turn the thorn of pain into her breast; it would make it easier to be certain, to hear it from his own lips. Not knowing, guessing, was the worst part of the pain.

'Once upon a time,' he said impatiently, frowning. 'But I told you, it was over long ago.'

'And how long did it last?' she asked bitterly. 'How long do any of your affairs last? You get bored so easily.'

Nick gave a short sigh. 'In the past I have, I can't deny it. I don't lead a settled, stable life, I'm always moving from place to place, from country to country, and I'm a busy man. I have little time for a private life, I snatch a few hours where I can...that's why I've never married or had a long relationship with anyone.'

He turned to stare out of the limousine window at the brilliantly lit shops past which they were driving, and Gina bit her lip, too unhappy to have anything to say. He was telling her what she knew already—that any relationship they might have was doomed before it started. Love did not have a place in Nick's busy international jet-setting life.

'This time it's different,' he suddenly burst out. 'I didn't even realise how different until I left to go to Luxembourg. I had so much work to do, a very important board meeting to conduct, some complicated matters to discuss, decisions to make—and for the first time in my life I couldn't keep my mind on what I was doing. I kept thinking about you, wondering where you were, who you were with!' He was talking in a deep, rapid voice, his head bent so that she had to strain to hear him, and then he threw back his head and looked at her, his eyes brilliant, glittering.

She was almost frightened of that look, the demand and insistence of it.

'Don't!' she whispered and Nick put out a hand to her, a pleading gesture.

'If I don't get you into bed soon I'll go mad.'

She went white, trembling. 'I told you—I won't go to bed with you!'

Nick turned his head away again, his hand curling into a fist, and for a second there was silence, then he turned back and said quietly, 'Will you marry me, Gina?'

Gina couldn't breathe. She stared at him incredulously, her green eyes enormous in a face which had turned white.

'You're out of your mind!' she said, trying to work out his motives for that amazing proposal. Whatever it was, it wasn't love; he still wasn't talking about love and she didn't want anything else from him.

'Yes,' he said, to her surprise and laughed furiously. 'You're right—at the moment I'm out of my mind. Nothing like you has ever hit me before, I'm suffering, and I can't stand it. I've got to do something about it.'

'You make me sound like a disease!' she said crossly.

'It feels like an illness. Yes!' he said. 'I'm actually running a fever.' He threw out his hand, grabbed hers and lifted it to his forehead. 'Feel it!'

She pulled her hand away. She did not want him touching her. The lightest brush of his fingers made her pulses beat too fast.

'Don't be absurd!' She gave him a suspicious look. 'Have you been drinking?'

'Do you think I would have to be drunk before I proposed? No, I'm sober, and I'm being eminently practical, Gina. Look, I have a multi-national company to run. I can't afford to be distracted from business. For one thing, my schedule has been drawn up for the next year, I can already tell you what I'll be doing in two months, four, six . . . I know more or less where I will be every day, barring accidents or sudden changes of plan. I don't have any time to waste. You are a problem; I have to deal with the problem quickly and then I'll be free to get on with my life.'

'If I'm a problem, the solution's easy! Stay away from me!' she said, flushed and furious.

'That won't work,' he muttered, as if he had already considered that solution. 'It won't stop me thinking about you . . .'

She was having difficulty breathing. Had she been as much on his mind as he had been on hers? Oh, but even if she had . . . why had she? What did he really feel? She bitterly wished she knew him well enough to be sure of that.

'And I don't want you seeing other men,' he bit out.

There was a strange, crazy logic behind what he said, she thought with a pang of desolation. Marrying her was the cure to an annoying distraction from his more important life, his work, the only thing that really mattered, and if Nick married her it would stop her seeing other men.

She knew he couldn't be jealous. He was simply determined to add her—and through her full control of the *Sentinel*—to his possessions, and if she married someone else it would be a nuisance, and possibly a threat, to him.

Nick was watching her intently, trying to read the thoughts that lay behind her troubled face. She looked away from him, her eyes fixed on the chauffeur's dark cap. He was driving discreetly, his eyes staring straight ahead, and she knew that with the soundproof window closed between him and the passenger seats he could not hear a word they said, but she hoped he didn't occasionally glance at their reflection in his driving mirror. Their body language, their expressions, would probably be very betraying.

'Well?' Nick ground out. 'Gina…stop tormenting me, say yes!'

'I can't!' she whispered.

He turned towards her, his face darkly flushed. 'Give me one good reason!'

'We hardly know each other!'

'We've known each other for months!'

'Weeks!' she protested.

'It only took one look,' Nick said. 'I told you—the first time I saw you, at Barbary Wharf that day, I felt as if I had been pole-axed. I didn't realise how badly I'd got it for quite a time, but I knew what had happened to me, Gina, and so did you, didn't you?'

She was afraid to admit anything, she needed time to think, to work out the wisest thing to do, so she shook her head, her green eyes misty and uneasy.

'Don't lie!' Nick snarled, and made one of his hawklike swoops, his hand closing on her neck as she tried to pull back, avoid him. His mouth searched hungrily for hers, she twisted and turned, terrified that if he kissed her she would never have the strength to reject him. Nick made a fierce noise and pushed her back against the deep upholstery of the Rolls, his lips hot and possessive as they came down on hers.

She tried not to let him get to her, but it was a hopeless struggle. The kiss blotted out everything but the desire raging between them; she gave a moan of surrender, suddenly so weak that her bones seemed to have melted inside her overheated flesh. She tried once more to remember all her reasons for distrusting him, but none of them seemed to matter, compared to the wild compulsion of her own emotions, the demand and fire of his.

They were so absorbed, they didn't even notice the car slowing, purring to a halt, until the engine sound shut off altogether and silence fell.

Then Nick drew back, breathing thickly, and Gina forced open drowsy green eyes to stare at him; neither of them said anything, they just looked at each other, passion pulsing between them.

'Say yes,' he muttered, his eyes hot.

She almost did, her mind in utter confusion, and then it cleared a little, and she sighed, frowning. 'I can't, just like that...I need to think!'

'There's nothing to think about!' he said between his teeth, his black brows together and a furious colour in his face.

Gina shot a look at the chauffeur, afraid he might be watching them in his driving-mirror, but the man was staring sideways at the house as if admiring the design

of it. These streets held some of the most coveted houses
in London, and some of the most expensive.

There was a light showing underneath the canopy of
the porch, as usual at night, but the rest of the house
was dark, except for Sir George's window, which showed
a soft pinkish glow. He must be reading in bed.

'Gina!' Nick whispered, and she looked back at him,
shaking her head.

'I'm trying to think! Don't try to stampede me!'

'I have to stampede you,' he said, his mouth twisting.
'I want this settled, I want to get married immediately.
I've had enough of waiting around, of frustration and
uncertainty.' He put out a hand and touched her cheek
gently, his fingertips caressing, his eyes passionately
intent. 'You want me as much as I want you, don't you?
Do you think I don't know that? Every time we kiss the
feeling gets stronger—what is there to think about?'

'The things you're just pushing aside,' Gina said
huskily. 'You keep telling me not to think, and I have
to ask myself why you don't want me to! Why the hurry,
all this urgency?'

He looked at her, his eyes glittering, and her heart
gave a convulsive leap. 'Don't you know?' he said in a
deep, rough voice, and panic spread inside her like a
forest fire running in tongues of flame through dry
undergrowth. 'You won't sleep with me otherwise—
marriage is the only option you'll allow me.'

Her lips were as dry as bone, she ran a tongue tip over
them and he watched, as if hypnotised, his own lips
apart, his breathing audible.

She swallowed and made herself think. 'I need to be
sure you aren't just marrying me to get hold of the Tyrrell
shares,' she said, and saw his eyes flicker.

It was a tiny betrayal, and he immediately looked away, his lids down over those hard grey eyes as if to hide that brief reaction, but he was too late; she had seen it, and a chill seeped into her.

He might keep telling her he wanted her, and there was some truth in it, some fire behind all the smoke he was trying to blind her with, because Nick hadn't been pretending just now, when he kissed her and touched her. Unless he was the best actor in the world that had been real passion, an urgent frustration he showed her— but he had other motives too, underneath the drive of his desire.

He wanted complete control of the *Sentinel*. He did not want to share it with anyone else, either Sir George or her. Everything she knew about Nick told her that he had to win, to own, to possess—in her case, his need for all those things was complex, fragmented.

He wanted her body, but he wanted her inheritance, too, and she had a cold suspicion he wanted the *Sentinel* more than he wanted her.

'Do you know how many papers I own?' he asked her drily, with a curl of his mouth which mocked her. 'I've already spent far more time on this London operation than I should have done—I have a lot of other irons in the fire at the moment, I should be in Luxembourg again next week and then Athens for a meeting with Alex Gregaros, my Greek partner, over costs and profits, and after that Paris, where we're opening a new magazine in the spring.'

'Yes, I know how busy and important you are,' Gina angrily said. 'But I also know you still want majority control of the *Sentinel*, and to get it you need me.'

He was looking irritated now. 'Gina, I run a huge multi-national, and the London operation isn't even as important as some others in the group. I was late getting into the English field, because I had such trouble getting hold of an English national paper to flagship the provincial papers I'm picking up.'

Her eyes widened—what provincial papers? Was he buying even more English papers, then? She hadn't realised the extent of his English ambitions until then.

He gave her a sardonic smile. 'You don't really think I am desperate to get the rest of Sir George's shares? I already have effectual control of the *Sentinel*. My shares match Sir George's, and he is no longer trying to oppose me, so the board vote the way I want them to! Why on earth should I marry you just to get hold of the Tyrrell shares?'

'Because you can never rest until you are in complete control!' she accused fiercely.

Nick stared at her in grim silence for a moment. 'You just don't trust me,' he said slowly, his voice freezing over.

She didn't answer, she didn't need to, the admission was in her face, and she was close to tears because she wanted to believe him, to trust him, but she couldn't.

Nick straightened, his face dark and shuttered now, anger in every movement he made, in the very way he breathed.

'You're turning me down?'

He didn't shout, but she flinched at the leashed force in his voice.

'I . . .'

'Yes or no?' he grated, eyes like daggers.

She swallowed, and said, 'I'm sorry.'

For a moment she thought he might even hit her, but instead he turned and flung the door of the limousine open, got out himself and turned to help her down. She was afraid to let him touch her again, however formally; so she ignored his hand and stumbled out unaided, trembling so much that she could hardly walk straight.

'Goodnight, thank you for the lift home...' she began, but Nick was already back in the limousine, the door slamming behind him. Gina hurried up the steps into the porch and unlocked the front door with shaky hands. As she stepped over the threshold she heard the Rolls-Royce move off; looking round she caught one glimpse of the tail-lights, then it was gone and the street was silent again.

She had never seen him so angry. He had often been impatient, furious, insistent before, but this had been different—a white-hot, deadly rage which made her shiver every time she remembered the look on his face. She had hit him where it hurt Nick most: in his masculinity.

He had not asked her to marry him lightly; he hadn't wanted to get married at all, he had made that brutally plain. But he had proposed! And it obviously hadn't even entered his head that she might refuse. She didn't think she would ever forget that look in his eyes as it dawned on him that she was rejecting him.

She had often wondered what made Nick tick, and she thought she knew now—he needed to win, to beat down opposition, to keep adding to his possessions. Nick was an achiever, fixated on success. Tonight she had turned him down; she had, in Nick's terms, been the winner in the power struggle between them. Nick had failed. He had lost. That was why he had been so violently angry, so stunned and incredulous.

She bolted for her bedroom and locked the door before the tears came, cascading down her white face, her body shaking with sobs she had to stifle in her pillow in case the old man heard her. It was some time before she could bring herself to get up and undress; and then she moved unsteadily around, stripping off her clothes, washing, putting on her nightdress.

It was very late before she fell asleep, and when her alarm clock shrilled she woke with jangled nerves, sitting up in bed with a pale face and shadowed eyes, her mind already filling with bitter memories of the night before.

Sir George gave her a frowning stare at the breakfast table. 'What time did you come in last night?'

'I was in by midnight, but I couldn't sleep,' she said, sipping orange juice.

She could not face any of the cooked food the housekeeper had prepared. She might manage a piece of toast, nothing more.

'Why?' barked Sir George and she looked blankly at him.

'Why what?'

'Why couldn't you sleep? Something on your mind?'

She couldn't stop the colour stealing up her face, and looked away.

The old man chuckled. 'Don't tell me you're getting serious about the Dutchman?'

Gina was relieved that he thought it was Piet keeping her awake, so she laughed a little feverishly and gave an honest, if an evasive answer.

'He's charming.'

'Hmm...' said Sir George. 'Clever, I grant you that, and pleasant enough—but he isn't ever going to set the world on fire.' He paused, then hurriedly said, 'I'm not trying to interfere, don't think that!'

'Oh, no,' she said with demure amusement, and met his eyes.

The old man was forced to laugh, then he said with his usual embarrassment when he discussed personal subjects like his own feelings, 'I care what happens to you, my dear, I only want you to be happy, and it is a long time since James died. I don't expect you to grieve for the rest of your life...'

'I will,' she said quietly. 'I loved James very much, and I will always grieve and miss him, but I'm alive, and I'm human...'

'I know you are,' the old man said huskily. 'You will fall in love again, Gina, you're young, you have plenty of time... but this Dutchman—charming as he may be, I'm not sure he's the right man for you.'

She smiled wryly back; she knew he was right and wondered what he would say if he knew that Nick had proposed to her last night. Sir George would be delighted at the prospect of her marrying the head of Caspian International—in his eyes it would mean that through her the Tyrrells would be getting the *Sentinel* back! She shuddered to imagine his face if he ever found out she had turned Nick down!

That lunchtime, Gina and Hazel ate in the office canteen to save time. 'For the last time, thank heavens!' Hazel gloomily said, contemplating her meal.

Gina had chosen the stir-fried rice dish which was the dish of the day, and was enjoying it. 'You should have had this!' she said and Hazel nodded.

'I'm dieting, though, so I picked salad, and look at it! I'm sure this is left over from yesterday or the day before!'

'Take it back and complain!'

Hazel grimaced. 'I can't be bothered. I'm not hungry, anyway.' She pushed the tired lettuce aside to find a slice of tomato, which she ate, then said casually, 'Did you have a good time last night?'

For a moment Gina was bewildered, looking up at her. 'Last night?'

'The film première!'

'Oh. Yes, it was very good, you must go and see it.'

'Did Piet enjoy it?' Hazel asked in her usual offhand tone when talking about Piet.

'I think so,' Gina said, more interested in her lunch.

'You're seeing a lot of him, aren't you?' Hazel asked abruptly. 'Is it serious?'

Gina didn't look up but she was alerted by Hazel's voice, and spoke carefully. 'He's a very nice man, I like him, we get on well—but neither of us is serious. We aren't romantic about each other, I mean.'

Hazel laughed shortly. 'I don't believe in platonic affairs.'

'This isn't an affair. It's friendship and it will never be anything more. We aren't interested in each other that way.' Gina urgently wanted to make Hazel believe her.

'But you keep dating each other!' was all Hazel said.

'We don't date—we just keep each other company. It's more fun than going out alone.' Gina hesitated, then said shyly, 'Hazel, I'm interested in someone else; I'm not in the least interested in Piet that way...'

Hazel's frown deepened. 'Does he know that?'

'Piet isn't interested in me, either,' Gina said. 'We haven't talked about it, but I'm sure he is interested in someone else, too.'

'Who?' Hazel asked huskily.

'Ask him,' Gina gently suggested, and Hazel went dark red.

'Certainly not!'

CHAPTER NINE

THE Old City Hotel had been built in the days when rococo decoration was all the rage, and under the shabbiness and neglect an air of grandeur still breathed from the vast, echoing ballroom with its gilded cherubs, marble pillars, great gilt-framed mirrors and ornate ceilings.

The *Sentinel* staff sat at small marble-topped tables around the floor, and for twenty minutes nobody danced, they just sat staring at the décor, listening to the music, talking.

Dinner had been a lengthy affair, with speech after speech from the top table at which sat Sir George, the editor, Harry Dearden, who was retiring that week, and Joe Mackinlay, the managing director who was also leaving, with a number of other heads of departments. The meal was quite good, if conventional: soup followed by a slice of poached white fish, then roast beef, followed by lemon mousse. Wine flowed freely, courtesy of the management, and with coffee everyone was offered a liqueur, so by the time they began to wander through the double doors into the Edwardian ballroom they were all in a mood to enjoy themselves, but faintly lethargic.

Sir George waited for a while, then, to get them all on their feet, opened the dancing, picking as his partner the elderly lady who had been bringing tea around the director's floor for forty years. She was retiring, too. Looking around the softly lit ballroom, Gina lost count of the number of people who had been made redundant. No wonder Sir George looked tired. This had been an exhausting and depressing week for him. He had worked in the old Fleet Street building since he left college, more than fifty years ago, and the Tyrrell family had built it. Leaving it was more of a wrench than the old man had ever bargained for, especially in these circumstances, with control of the newspaper going into other hands.

Gina knew many of the people she saw. Working for the proprietor had meant coming into contact at one time or another with most departments, and gave her a strong sense of the family nature, until now, of the business.

When Sir George left, she realised, life on the *Sentinel* would never be the same. No doubt the Caspian organisation was efficient and many aspects of work and pay might be better, but on a human level something important would be lost, a real sense of identity.

She looked back at Sir George, revolving in a stately way on the dance-floor, and caught sight of Hazel and Piet dancing just behind him, their bodies not quite touching. Gina smiled impulsively. That looked hopeful. She had begun to think she was going to have to draw them a diagram!

The nearest table to her held the star staff of the paper: the leader writers, the columnists, all trying to talk each other down.

Beyond them sat Daniel Bruneille, and the rest of the staff who worked on the foreign desk—Roz among them, slender and striking in a dress like a flamenco dancer's: tight-bodiced, low-necked, tight-waisted, but with a full, layered, flouncing scarlet skirt.

'Come and join us!' she called, catching Gina's eye.

'Later!' she promised. She had to stay with Sir George until he chose to go to bed, as he probably would quite soon. He was usually heavy-eyed by ten-thirty.

'Don't forget!' Roz said. Her face was flushed and there was an angry sparkle to her eye which was increasingly familiar whenever she was anywhere near Daniel Bruneille. He was a thorn in Roz's side, and Gina could sympathise—men like Daniel, and Nick Caspian, were hard to live with and harder to forget. Roz wasn't Daniel Bruneille's idea of a woman, obviously; he preferred the ultra-feminine type, gentle and yielding. Maybe Frenchmen all did? Gina didn't know France well enough to guess. One thing she did know—Roz was a good journalist and a strong woman. Daniel Bruneille was not going to find it easy to beat Roz down or get her out of the foreign department. Roz had a father to live up to—and battles to win.

'May I have this dance?' Joe Mackinlay asked, bending over to speak to her.

'I'd love to, thank you, Joe,' she smiled, getting up with a rustle of amber silk.

Her floor-length evening dress glowed against her pale skin and deepened the colour of the russet hair piled high on her head, held there by black velvet and a band of pearls. She had bought the dress especially for this occasion, loving the colour but hesitating briefly because the neckline plunged rather recklessly, and she was very modest.

In the end she couldn't resist the dress, deciding she could wear a heavy Victorian necklace of amber and gold with it, which would fill the neckline and cover up some of her exposed skin. It was one of the Tyrrell family jewels. She had never worn it before because it could only be worn at night, on such an occasion—it was far too large and ornate to wear except with evening dress, so she was quite pleased to have an excuse for getting it out of the safe.

'What are you going to do now, Joe?' she asked her partner, who smiled down at her.

'My wife wants to sell our London house and move back up to Scotland to be nearer her family, so we'll probably do that, and I'll fish and do a lot of walking—that was always what we did for holidays, our favourite way of passing the time. I don't know if I'll like being on permanent holiday, mind.'

'Sir George will miss you,' said Gina with sympathy, because she liked Joe Mackinlay, and his face brightened.

'I shall miss him, and everyone else I've worked with—it has come so suddenly, this retirement. I wasn't ready for it in my mind.' He lowered his voice and whispered, 'It's all that damned Caspian!'

She laughed. 'Yes, I'm afraid you're right.'

'Still, there's no point in crying over spilt milk—he's like death and taxes, you can't beat him so you might as well accept it.'

She shivered, hearing echoes in what he had said. Joe looked at her in surprise.

'A ghost walked over my grave,' she said in what she tried to make a light tone.

They swirled past Hazel and Piet, but neither of them had eyes for Gina. They were dancing in silence, their bodies moving in smooth harmony.

The music ended, and Piet's arm dropped slowly; he looked down at Hazel who was very flushed, her eyes bright.

'I might have known you would dance perfectly,' Piet said with wry amusement, and saw her eyes cloud over, her face stiffen again.

Hazel turned away, not wanting him to see how much he had hurt her, but Piet caught her hand.

'No, don't go cold on me again, I put that badly, I was only trying to say how much I enjoyed dancing with you.'

'You're always making fun of me,' Hazel said huskily, her eyes lowered.

They were the last off the floor and she felt conspicuous, she was sure people were staring, she heard laughter and thought it was aimed at her. Ever since she met Piet van Leyden her self-confidence had taken a knock—she had become intensely self-conscious.

Embarrassed, she pulled herself free and walked blindly out of the ballroom, not sure where she was going. She didn't realise Piet had followed her until she halted in an empty corridor to look about her for the powder-room, and Piet almost cannoned into her.

Hazel looked, startled, and glared at him. 'Go away!'

Piet glared back. 'You are the most contrary woman I have ever known!'

'Good,' Hazel said with fierce satisfaction. 'At least you can't ignore me now.'

'Ignore you? When did I ever manage to do that?' he snorted.

'When we first met. You stared right through me. I was the invisible woman as far as you were concerned.'

He stared at her, his blue eyes baffled. 'What on earth are you talking about?'

'You see! You don't even remember. It was in Selfridges, one lunchtime.' She curled her lip at him. 'I was with Gina, and you couldn't take your eyes off her long enough to notice me.'

He grimaced. 'Ah.' He smiled down at her, his mouth crooked. 'I had met her first, you see, with Sir George at Barbary Wharf. She was so lovely, a glamorous redhead with sad eyes...'

'I don't want to hear about it!' Hazel said furiously. 'Go back inside and dance with her and leave me alone!'

'Gina is a very nice girl, and I'm fond of her,' said Piet with quiet patience. 'But when we got to know each other, we both realised there was no spark between us. You know what I mean?'

Hazel's face changed, her grey eyes wide and uncertain. It was exactly what Gina had told her, but she had not quite believed it then.

Piet put out a hand to her, fingers splayed. 'Touch me and feel it!' he whispered.

'Feel what?' Hazel whispered back, but at the same time her hand lifted to touch his, palm to warm palm, finger to finger.

'The spark,' Piet said, and they both felt it leaping between them, the electricity of their instinctive reaction to each other. Their eyes held, Hazel began to tremble and Piet bent slowly towards her, looking at her parted mouth, then the swing doors of the ballroom noisily opened and several people came out talking loudly.

Hazel and Piet sprang apart and turned their backs to the intruders, pretending to study some sporting prints which hung nearby on the wall.

One of the newcomers had caught a glimpse of them before they had time to move, and she began to giggle, nudging her friends and whispering. Hazel blushed hotly, not daring to look at Piet. Another instant and he would have kissed her, and her heart beat heavily against her ribs. Oh, if only that noisy crowd would clear off!

Back in the ballroom, Gina smiled lovingly at Sir George. 'Enjoying yourself?'

'Yes, I am,' he said, with obvious surprise. 'You know, there are people here tonight that I haven't seen for years.'

She laughed. 'Well, I suppose in a big organisation like ours you must employ far more people than you ever get to meet.'

'Of course, but what I meant is that there are people here tonight who I know well, but rarely see now. Molly Lynn, for instance, been on the paper heaven knows how long—but it must be ten years since I last saw her! I've got out of touch, that's what it is! The firm was just too big for one man to be able to keep his finger on the pulse of it.'

'You did your best!' protested Gina, and he smiled at her wryly.

'Thank you, my dear. I think I did, but it wasn't good enough. Makes you wonder how Caspian manages to hold that empire of his together—not just thousands of people working for him, but all those different countries. How does he keep in touch with what is going on?'

One of the directors, Lord Hampden, gave a cynical laugh. 'Caspian has a team of professional people-watchers working for him, keeping him abreast of everything that is happening. He gets daily reports from all his companies; digests of company accounts and sales figures, everything he needs to know, plus private information about unions, staff changes, local problems. And he reads it all!'

Sir George looked along the table to where Nick was talking to one of the other directors. 'He isn't human!'

Lowering his voice, Lord Hampden muttered, grinning, 'Think he's a robot? Some sort of extra-terrestrial come to take over our planet?'

Sir George laughed loudly. 'Probably.' Then his eyes narrowed on Nick again and he frowned. 'He's been talking to young Slade for half an hour! Wonder what he's up to?'

'Nothing good, you can be certain!' said Lord Hampden, as a ladies excuse me dance was announced from the orchestra. Lady Hampden got up and held out her hand to him, and her husband groaned. 'Must I?' But he obediently rose to his feet and followed her on to the floor.

Sir George looked sideways at Gina, and whispered to her, 'Go and break that up, will you, my dear?'

She stared back, bewildered. 'What?'

Impatiently, the old man said, 'Get Nick away from young Slade and give me a chance to find out what Nick has been saying to the boy!'

Gina flushed a delicate pink. 'How am I supposed to do that? I can't just interrupt...'

'Ask Nick to dance!' Sir George commanded in a low tone. 'That is what we are all here for, after all! He shouldn't be talking business, he should be paying attention to the staff. Ask him to dance and tell him to go and dance with one of the secretaries after you.'

Gina hesitated, biting her lip. 'I...I can't do that!'

'Of course you can!' said Sir George impatiently.

She had managed to steer clear of Nick so far this evening. They had sat at the same table at dinner, but she had been placed far enough away from him to be able to ignore him without seeming rude.

All the same she had been able to observe Nick secretly from a distance, and realised that he must be feeling the strain of these last few days as well. He seemed increasingly tense, pale-skinned, his grey eyes very dark, his mouth a hard, white line. The elegance of his evening dress couldn't hide the controlled threat of the body under it. Nick was in no party mood, any more than she was!

'Well, go along!' Sir George said impatiently, frowning. 'I know you don't like the fellow, neither do I, but young Slade inherited around eight per cent of the shares from his father, and I don't want Caspian talking him into selling it. Luckily, the estate is still in probate, and young Slade can't sell them yet.'

'But I thought that when you sold him your shares it had been agreed that he wouldn't try to acquire any more, and would be content with a managing control?' Gina said, feeling faintly sick.

'He made all sorts of promises, but I know the man now. He wants a controlling majority, not a fifty-fifty share, as we have now. If he can talk young Slade into selling to him when he takes possession of his inheritance, he will, I'm certain of it!' Sir George looked down into her pale, fine-drawn features and sighed. 'Don't look so worried, my dear; I'll make sure Caspian doesn't get his hands on any more of the company. I've known young Slade since he was in his pram, I have had a very happy working relationship with his father and his grandfather before that—the boy won't sell me out to Caspian, however high the price!'

Gina forced a smile. 'No, I'm sure he won't.' She got up, feeling faintly shaky, and took a deep breath, then walked as steadily as she could towards where Nick was talking to Philip Slade.

Both men paused as she approached and looked round at her. Nick curved one sardonic eyebrow. 'Want me?' he asked in a tone which made her stiffen.

Philip Slade smiled at her. He was in his early twenties, but looked even younger because he had a very boyish face and body; slim, smooth-skinned, with soft, brown hair, and blue eyes which were light, very bright and held charm. His mouth was weak, though, Gina thought, smiling back at him.

'Enjoying the dance?' she asked, adding pointedly, 'That is what we are here for—to dance and enjoy ourselves. Have you danced yet, Mr Caspian?'

Nick acknowledged the deliberate formality by giving her a mocking glance, his mouth twisting. 'No, Mrs Tyrrell, I haven't.' He got to his feet and offered her his hand. 'May I have the pleasure of a dance with you?'

Feeling Sir George watching approvingly, she accepted his hand, her nerves quivering as their skin touched. Little beads of perspiration sprang out on her nape, under her hair. Any second now she would be in Nick's arms; close to him, touching him. She didn't know how she was going to bear it.

Nick's hand slid round her waist and drew her towards him; her waist bent under his hand, supple and yielding, and she sighed helplessly.

The music was meltingly sweet, a swirling waltz to which the dancers moved around them; the men in black evening dress, the girls in silk and lace and velvet, rustling skirts which flared out as they were spun around. Over Nick's shoulder she caught a glimpse of Hazel, in a rose-pink dress with a low-cut neckline, dancing with Piet again. Gina's brows rose steeply as Piet lowered his cheek and brushed it softly against Hazel's.

Well! That was fast work! Only that morning Piet and Hazel had been sniping at each other as usual, but one look at Hazel's flushed face told Gina that something drastic had happened in the last hour or so.

'That dress is enchanting,' Piet was whispering to Hazel, who let her hand stray along his shoulder to touch the bare nape of his neck.

He made a husky groaning sound. 'Mmm...do that again.'

She laughed softly. 'Later.'

'How soon can we leave this party?' asked Piet.

'Not yet,' Hazel said, but her body swayed closer and his arm tightened on her waist.

Gina watched them, half smiling. I can't wait to get Hazel alone to hear all about it, she thought, then felt Nick looking down at her, his black brows arched.

'Why the Mona Lisa smile? Are you plotting something?'

She raised wide, misty green eyes to him. 'Of course not—are you getting paranoid?'

'Probably,' he said, and grinned briefly. 'Sir George ordered you to ask me to dance, of course.'

'He thought it was time you did your duty,' she admitted, and got one of Nick's taunting smiles.

'He wasn't trying to stop me talking to Phil Slade?'

How did he always know what was in people's minds? she wondered, her mouth compressed. Was it telepathy, or a form of empathy, an ability to put himself in their place? Or sheer black magic, the power to eavesdrop on the thoughts of others, to sense what they would do before they knew themselves? Whatever power he used, it disturbed her. It made him frighteningly intelligent.

'He always dances with someone from each department,' she said, which was true, if evasive. 'He thought perhaps you didn't realise that that was what everyone expected of you. The women are all sitting there wondering when you're going to dance—and who with! When we've had our dance, he wants you to ask one of

the secretaries to dance, then work your way through
editorial, advertising, and so on.'

'I was going to do that in a moment,' Nick said, then
looked over her shoulder, his mouth curling in a dry
little smile. What was he staring at?

She glanced into one of the ornately framed mirrors
and saw that he was staring at Sir George, who was now
talking to Philip Slade. Another mirror was reflected,
behind them; she felt unreal suddenly, seeing an endless
vista of reflecting mirrors, each one holding a reflection
of another, making her a dancing shadow further and
further away, the chandeliers glittering overhead and the
other dancers smiling and swaying around her.

She shivered, stumbling, and Nick looked down, his
arm tightening on her waist.

Their eyes met. His dazzled her, like Arctic ice in the
sun. He stared deep into her green eyes and her head
spun; she had to cling on to his smooth shoulder to stay
upright. Everything around them vanished and they
moved together in a strange, tense silence, their bodies
in harmony, and yet in bitter conflict. The demand of
Nick's body pulsed against hers and Gina fought not to
feel the same aching need.

'I can't go on like this,' he whispered, and she pretended not to know what he meant.

'Shall we sit down, then?' she asked, trying to pull
away.

He caught her back. 'You know what I mean!'

'Don't, Nick!' she said, afraid to fight him while they
were on that very public ballroom floor, watched by so
many members of the *Sentinel* staff.

'Gina,' he whispered, holding her so close that she
could scarcely breathe, and began to shake.

Nick made a hoarse sound, wordless, angry, pleading; and then his cheek moved against hers, she felt the heat of his skin and under that the hard tension of the bones. He moved his face backwards and forwards against her own, sighing.

'Stop it, people will start staring,' she muttered, afraid to lift her eyes for fear of meeting curiosity or amusement in the other faces around them.

Nick was indifferent to any audience they might have. 'I've got to have you,' he muttered into her ear. 'All my life I've wanted something, that's the way I'm made, I've always been chasing something…this company, that company.'

'That's all you care about!' she angrily said.

'It was once,' he admitted. 'I certainly know how it feels to want something so badly it's a permanent ache inside you. One day I'll tell you why. I grew up in a hard school, Gina. I learnt to be tenacious, to wait and plan and hang on until I got what I wanted. But I've never wanted to take over a company as much as I want you.'

'Am I supposed to be flattered? You're talking about me as if I were a thing, a possession to be bought or grabbed or traded!'

'That isn't how I think of you!' His voice deepened, rough and husky. 'For weeks I haven't been able to sleep or think or work, and I can't bear to live like this much longer! It's making me violent.'

'You're scaring me,' she whispered, afraid to look around in case everyone in the vast ballroom was watching them.

Nick was keeping his voice so low that she could barely hear him, and she doubted if anyone else could, but their body language was probably very easy to read, as they moved together, to the music and yet at the same time to another rhythm altogether, the rhythm of desire.

'I don't want to scare you,' he huskily murmured, his lips touching her lobe and making her ears beat with the drum of her own blood. 'Life is too short to waste—don't be a coward, Gina. Time won't stand still for you. Grab your happiness while you can. What are you afraid of? All I want is to love you, and teach you to love me.'

Her eyes were misty with unshed tears. 'I wish I could believe you...' she breathed, and Nick's arms tightened on her waist.

'You can,' he muttered, and buried his mouth in the side of her throat.

A long, aroused shudder ran through her and she had to bite her inner lip to silence a moan of pleasure.

'Oh...Nick...'

She felt herself collapsing inwards. She had longed for weeks now to surrender herself to him, to stop fighting him and herself, and at that instant nothing mattered except Nick; the compulsion to love was stronger than anything else in life.

Nick lifted his head and looked down at her, his eyes brilliant, fierce. Gina couldn't hold that look, she gave a long, wild sigh and hid her flushed face on his shoulder.

Nick breathed audibly. 'How soon can we get away from here?' he asked and then the music stopped and everyone started clapping before drifting back to their tables.

Nick kept an arm around her waist. 'When can we make an excuse and leave?' he asked urgently, as they walked back towards where Sir George was standing, beside the table, watching them, his jaw thrust out, his head lowered, like a bull about to charge.

'We can't!' Gina said, worried by the way the old man stood there. 'Sir George will expect both of us to stay until the last dance of the evening! He always does.'

'Let him! I need you more than he does, tonight.' Nick had a triumphant glitter around him suddenly, and her heart turned over with love and defiance. He was right, wasn't he? Life was too short to waste.

'Well . . . maybe . . .' she murmured uncertainly.

She and Nick came to a stop as they reached the table and saw Sir George's expression at close quarters. Gina took a deep, shaken breath. Why was the old man looking like that? Nick's smile went and a wariness took its place.

The old man stared at him, breathing audibly, squaring up to Nick. 'You slippery swine,' he broke out after a moment. 'I might have known you would cheat me somehow! If I'd realised that probate had been granted on that will I would have seen to it that young Slade sold to me, but he never told me he was so desperate for money, and you and I had an agreement, dammit! You know it was understood . . . no, dammit! You swore you wouldn't try to buy any more shares if I agreed to sell you enough to give us joint control—and then, you lying, sneaking cur, you went behind my back, didn't you? And now you have the majority, you control the *Sentinel* and——'

He broke off, seeming incapable of getting out another word, choking and spluttering, his face dark red, his eyes bulging.

'Sir George, don't!' Gina said anxiously, running to put an arm around him, but he pushed her away, and flung out an accusing hand at Nick, his fingers splayed.

'You always meant to get complete control, didn't you?' he bellowed, glaring.

'I had my reasons,' Nick said, smiling, and Gina gave him a stricken look, the colour draining from her face. He admitted it so coolly, he didn't care what the old man thought of him—what anybody thought!

Nick turned his head to look at her, and she stared back, white-faced.

'You have no scruples, do you?' she whispered. 'No morals, no scruples...no heart...'

'Don't be stupid, Gina, I did it for you,' Nick said, and that seemed to her the final straw.

'For me? For me, you liar?' she broke out, trembling, and hating him.

'Gina?' Sir George hoarsely said, a dawning comprehension in his face. 'What did he mean—he did it for you? What's been going on? How are you involved in this? You didn't tell me that you...you and him? My God...' He broke off abruptly, making a strange, hoarse, impeded sound, as if fighting for breath.

'What is it? Are you ill?' she anxiously began, but he didn't answer.

He clutched his chest, bent forwards convulsively, still making that awful noise. Gina tried to catch him as he fell, slowly, crumpling at the knees, but she was too late.

The events of the next few minutes were a blur to her. The old man lay on the ballroom floor, eyes closed, blue-lipped, breathing stertorously; she knelt beside him, tears in her eyes, holding his hand. Everyone else had crowded round and was staring, whispering. Nick began barking orders, telling someone to clear the room, sending somebody running to telephone for an ambulance, demanding blankets from the hotel manager.

'We must keep him warm,' his voice said from far away.

Gina couldn't take her eyes off the drawn, lined face of the old man. She felt for a pulse in that thin blue wrist, but couldn't find one, although she could hear the air being dragged so painfully in and out of the old man's lungs.

'What should we do?' she asked desperately, feeling totally helpless because she had no idea what they should be doing; and at that instant Sir George's loud breathing seemed to stop and Gina stared down at his sallow face in terror.

'Please don't die... Oh, God, please don't let him die...'

Nick knelt beside her, pushed her roughly out of the way. She watched in bewilderment as he yanked off the old man's tie, ripping his shirt open to the waist.

'What are you doing?' she sobbed, but Nick took no notice of her, discarding his own jacket and undoing his own tie. It was like a nightmare; Gina had no idea what was happening.

Dazedly, it dawned on her a few seconds later that he was giving Sir George artificial respiration, kneeling over him, with the muscles rippling under the elegant shirt, working on the old man until the sweat was running down his own face. She could hear Nick breathing now; he tried to breathe air back into the old man's body and she could only stand and watch, white-faced and dark-eyed.

The swing doors of the ballroom crashed back suddenly, and the ambulancemen came running in, but it was a doctor in a white coat who reached Sir George first. A young, skinny man with a pale face, he pushed Nick wordlessly aside and started examining Sir George. Nick stood up, his hands hanging at his side, his hair dishevelled, his breathing roughened by his exertion sounding very loud in the silent room.

'He isn't dead, say he isn't dead,' Gina pleaded.

'Take her out,' the doctor said over his shoulder, opening a cardiac arrest pack and beginning to make preparations to try to restore the old man's heartbeat.

'No, I want to stay!' Gina cried, determined not to leave the old man with strangers.

'Sorry, but I can't work with an audience. You must go out,' the doctor crisply said.

'Come along, Gina,' Nick said quietly, putting an arm round her to lead her out.

She hit out at him. 'Get away from me.'

'You're just in the way here.'

'My place is with him! He'll need me if... when...' She couldn't finish that sentence, her throat salty with tears. She couldn't believe the old man might have gone; she couldn't believe it.

Nick put a hand under her knees and before she could stop him picked her up without another word, ignoring her angry struggles, and carried her out of the ballroom.

A lot of the *Sentinel* staff were outside in the foyer, some standing in muted groups, some sitting on couches or chairs, talking quietly together, their eyes on the double doors into the ballroom. They all fell silent as Nick and Gina came out, and watched them fixedly. Piet and Hazel were the closest; right outside the door, their faces pale and anxious.

Nick let Gina slide to the floor, still keeping his arm around her to support her as she swayed, faintly dizzy.

She pushed his hand away, saw Piet and Hazel and ran to them like a terrified animal taking sanctuary. 'The old man...' she sobbed. 'I think he's dying...'

Hazel put an arm around her. 'They can work miracles these days, and they were here very quickly, I'm sure they'll...' Her voice died helplessly away. She looked at Piet over Gina's head, her face distressed, and he smiled reassurance at her.

'Better she sits down, I think,' Piet said, his voice very Dutch. 'Come, Gina, sit here, my dear. You will feel better sitting down. I will get you a glass of brandy, you need some Dutch courage, *ja*?' He smiled at her. 'Hazel will stay with you and take care of you.'

He vanished in the direction of the bar and came back a moment later with a glass which he insisted Gina should sip, although she tried to push it away. She took a few sips, shuddering at the heat of the alcohol, and then the glass shook in her hand as she heard the ballroom door open.

She couldn't bear to look round because she knew, she had known before she left the ballroom, she had known when Sir George's loud breathing stopped and never started again, but she did not want to believe what she knew. She wasn't ready to accept it, yet. She was trying to pretend it hadn't happened.

She heard the doctor talking in a low voice to Nick, and the ambulancemen carrying the stretcher away, through the ornate foyer, while throngs of *Sentinel* staff stood watching, in horrified silence.

Nick came over and said quietly, 'I think I should drive you home now; there's no point in you going with him, you know. I'm sorry, Gina, very sorry...'

She lifted her head with exhausted reluctance. Hazel kept an arm around her waist, as if afraid she might fall over if she let her stand alone.

Gina's darkened eyes met Nick's directly, and there was an enormous gulf between them now; uncrossable, an abyss.

He had been using her from the beginning; manipulating her, in his pursuit of a majority shareholding, while all the time he had been looking around in case he found some other way of getting what he wanted. When he knew Philip Slade could at last sell his shares he'd stepped in at once to buy them. His only interest in her had, after all, been the shares she would one day inherit. All his talk of love, of marriage, had been lies. She had never meant anything to him, but a means to an end. The chill realisation made her feel sick.

'He's dead,' she said aloud, to herself.

'I'm afraid so,' Nick said, watching her intently. She knew how clever he was; she realised that that brain of his was working rapidly, trying to guess which way she would jump, trying to forestall any move she made.

'He needn't have died,' she said, her voice a wisp of smoke, a thread of sound. 'He was murdered.'

There were gasps from everyone in earshot.

'You're in shock, Gina,' Nick said, his killer's eyes warily trying to pretend sympathy, concern. She knew better now. She knew how phoney his interest in her had always been. To all the people here, watching, listening, to anyone who did not know him as well as she knew him, it probably looked as if he really cared.

'This has been a terrible shock to all of us,' he said in that quiet, kind-sounding voice, and she wanted to scream at him. Liar, liar. 'But to you, most of all,' he said. 'The doctor has prescribed a sedative for you—he thinks you should go to bed and try to sleep. I'll drive you home now.'

'I don't want you to do anything for me!' she said in a calm, distant voice which was the worse for containing such hatred. 'You've done enough. You killed him.'

People gasped again, eyes rounded, they were all listening to everything that was said, but Gina did not care. She was too intent on hating Nick.

He had killed the old man. He had humiliated, cheated, betrayed her. But if he thought he was going to get away with it, unscathed himself, he was wrong. Somehow she would find a way of punishing him.

'I'll never forgive you,' she said. 'I never want to see you again.'

Nick didn't move, he stood there like a statue, his face carved and cold and blank.

She had nothing else to say. It was all said. She began to walk unsteadily towards the hotel entrance. She had to get away, away from the curious, staring, shaken faces, yet the only place she could go was back to that empty house.

'We must go with her, take her home,' Piet murmured to Hazel.

Hazel was very pale. 'Yes, she can't be left alone. I'll stay the night with her. But Sir George's car won't be here yet to pick them up—it was ordered for midnight. I wonder if there are taxis outside, or if we should ask the reception people to call one for us?'

'No, my car is in the car park,' said Piet. 'I'll run and get it and you can wait outside the hotel with her. I won't be two minutes, darling.'

He hurried off and Hazel caught up with Gina, who was standing outside on the pavement looking around in a dazed, uncertain way. Gently, Hazel said to her, 'Piet is getting his car. Shall we wait inside where it is warm? You ought to pick up your jacket from the cloakroom; you'll need it, it's quite a cool night.'

Gina didn't seem to hear her. She was trying to think, but her life had changed so suddenly that she still didn't believe it. She couldn't think ahead, make plans, even take in everything that this would mean.

One thing she was crystal-clear about, though. Somehow she was going to see to it that Nick Caspian paid for what he had done to the old man.

Don't miss *Battle for Possession*, Barbary Wharf Book Two.

Will Gina's and Nick's feelings for each other be vented through revenge and hatred, or passion and love? Will Hazel find room in her life—and her heart—for Piet? Will Roz be able to find true happiness? Find out in *Battle for Possession*, Barbary Wharf Book Two, coming next month from Harlequin Presents.

Coming Next Month

#1503   DESPERATE MEASURES Sara Craven
Philippa Roscoe needs money urgently—and *lots* of it. Alain de Courcy is prepared to supply it—at a price. What he wants is marriage—and not just in *name* only. Philippa has little choice but to go along with his conditions.

#1504   HEARTSONG Melinda Cross
When Madeline Chambers's dream of working with Elias Shepherd, the famous international film-score composer, finally comes true, she realizes she's created quite the myth about him. Elias is cold, hard and cynical, with no place in his heart for anything but music....

#1505   STORM OVER PARADISE Robyn Donald
Even after seven years, Dominic Maxwell's belief that Fenella is a mercenary, promiscuous female hasn't changed. Yet, for each of their sakes, they have to reach some understanding while she's on the tropical island of Fala'isi. But Dominic's arrogant assumptions about her are hard to take, especially when attraction flares between them.

#1506   SAFETY IN NUMBERS Sandra Field
Josh MacNeill knows plenty of women who'd be happy to have him as their husband. So why is he still hankering after Clem, a woman who's hated him since she was ten years old—a woman who, in any case, would not make the sort of wife he has in mind....

#1507   THE DEVIL HIS DUE Diana Hamilton
Seth had made it clear six years ago that he never wanted to see Kate again. So why is he now insisting that Kate handle the renovations to his precious home? Whatever his reasons, Kate's fiery nature won't let her be manipulated without a fight!

#1508   A FORBIDDEN LOVING Penny Jordan
Of course, Silas Jardine hasn't fallen in love with Hazel. He's just being pleasant because she's Katie's mother. Hazel thinks she can cope with Silas's presence in her life, but if time proves her wrong, she hopes Silas won't notice the effect he's had on her.

#1509   BATTLE FOR POSSESSION Charlotte Lamb
The Barbary Wharf six-book saga continues with Book Two, *Battle For Possession*. Daniel Bruneille is the head of the *Sentinel*'s Foreign Affairs desk and Roz Amery is a foreign affairs correspondent. He's bossy and dictatorial. She's fiercely ambitious and independent. When they clash, it's a battle for possession! And don't forget media tycoon Nick Caspian and his adversary, Gina Tyrrell. Will Gina survive the treachery of Nick's betrayal and the passion of his kiss...? Barbary Wharf is a romantic adventure you won't want to put down.

#1510   THAT MIDAS MAN Valerie Parv
Jill badly needs the promotion at work in order to finance her legal battle with her ex-husband—she must win custody of their daughter. To get the promotion, she has to interview mining engineer millionaire Michael Thorne—a man known to hate the press. Somehow Jill must get through to him.

Available in November wherever paperback books are sold, or through Harlequin Reader Service:

In the U.S.
P.O. Box 1397
Buffalo, NY
14240-1397

In Canada
P.O. Box 603
Fort Erie, Ontario
L2A 5X3

HARLEQUIN SUPERROMANCE®

A PLACE IN HER HEART...

Somewhere deep in the heart of every grown woman is the little girl she used to be....

In September, October and November 1992, the world of childhood and the world of love collide in six very special romance titles. Follow these six special heroines as they discover the sometimes heart-wrenching, always heartwarming joy of being a Big Sister.

Written by six of your favorite Superromance authors, these compelling and emotionally satisfying romantic stories will earn a place in your heart!

SEPTEMBER 1992

#514   NOTHING BUT TROUBLE—Sandra James
#515   ONE TO ONE—Marisa Carroll

OCTOBER 1992

#518   OUT ON A LIMB—Sally Bradford
#519   STAR SONG—Sandra Canfield

NOVEMBER 1992

#522   JUST BETWEEN US—Debbi Bedford
#523   MAKE-BELIEVE—Emma Merritt

AVAILABLE WHEREVER
HARLEQUIN SUPERROMANCE
BOOKS ARE SOLD

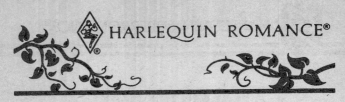

Harlequin Regency® Romance™

WHO SAYS ROMANCE IS A THING OF THE PAST?

We do! At Harlequin Regency Romance, we offer you romance the way it was always meant to be.

What could be more romantic than to follow the adventures of a duchess or duke through the glittering assembly rooms of Regency England? Or to eavesdrop on their witty conversations or romantic interludes? The music, the costumes, the ballrooms and the dance will sweep you away to a time when pleasure was a priority and privilege a prerequisite.

If you are longing for the good old days when falling in love still meant something very special, then come to Harlequin Regency Romance—romance with a touch of class.

RRG

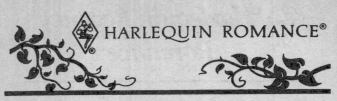

HARLEQUIN ROMANCE®

Valerie Bloomfield comes home to Orchard Valley, Oregon, for
the saddest of reasons. Her father has suffered a serious heart
attack, and now his three daughters are gathering at his side,
praying he'll survive.

Orchard Valley

This visit home will change Valerie's life—especially when
she meets Colby Winston, her father's handsome and
strong-willed doctor!

"The Orchard Valley trilogy features three delightful, spirited
sisters and a trio of equally fascinating men. The stories are rich
with the romance, warmth of heart and humor readers expect,
and invariably receive, from Debbie Macomber."

—Linda Lael Miller

Don't miss the Orchard Valley trilogy by Debbie Macomber:

VALERIE   Harlequin Romance #3232 (November 1992)
STEPHANIE   Harlequin Romance #3239 (December 1992)
NORAH   Harlequin Romance #3244 (January 1993)

Look for the special cover flash on each book!

Available wherever Harlequin books are sold   ORC-G

"BARBARY WHARF" SWEEPSTAKES
OFFICIAL RULES — NO PURCHASE NECESSARY

1. To enter each drawing complete the appropriate Offical Entry Form. Alternatively, you may enter any drawing by hand printing on a 3″ × 5″ card (mechanical reproductions are not acceptable) your name, address, daytime telephone number and prize for which that entry is being submitted (Wedgwood Tea Set, $1,000 Shopping Spree, Sterling Silver Candelabras, Royal Doulton China, Crabtree & Evelyn Gift Baskets or Sterling Silver Tray) and mailing it to: Barbary Wharf Sweepstakes, P.O. Box 1397, Buffalo, NY 14269-1397.

No responsibility is assumed for lost, late or misdirected mail. For eligibility all entries must be sent separately with first class postage affixed and be received by 11/23/92 for Wedgwood Tea Set (approx. value $543) or, at winner's option, $500 cash drawing; 12/22/92 for the $1,000 Shopping Spree at any retail establishment winner selects or, at winner's option, $1,000 cash drawing; 1/22/93 for Sterling Silver Candelabras (approx. value $875) or, at winner's option, $700 cash drawing, 2/22/93 for the Royal Doulton China service for 8 (approx. value $1,060) or, at winner's option, $900 cash drawing; 3/22/93 for the 12 monthly Crabtree & Evelyn Gift Baskets (approx. value $960) or, at winner's option, $750 cash drawing, and 4/22/93 for the Sterling Silver Tray (approx. value $1,200) or, at winner's option, $750 cash drawing. All winners will be selected in random drawings to be held within 7 days of each drawing eligibility deadline.

A random drawing from amongst all eligible entries received for participation in any or all drawings will be held no later than April 29, 1993 to award the Grand Prize of a 10 day trip for two (2) to London, England (approx. value $6,000) or, at winner's option, $6,000 cash. Travel option includes 10 nights accommodation at the Kensington Park Hotel, Continental breakfast daily, theater tickets for 2, plus round trip airfare and $1,000 spending money; air transportation is from commercial airport nearest winner's home; travel must be completed within 12 months of winner notification, and is subject to space and accommodation availability; travellers must sign and return a Release of Liability prior to traveling.

2. Sweepstakes offer is open only to residents of the U.S. (except Puerto Rico), and Canada who are 21 years of age or older, except employees and immediate family members of Torstar Corp., its affiliates, subsidiaries, and all agencies, entities and persons connected with the use, marketing, or conduct of this sweepstakes. All federal, state, provincial, municipal and local laws apply. Offer void wherever prohibited by law. Taxes and/or duties are the sole responsibility of the winner. Any litigation within the province of Quebec respecting the conduct and awarding of a prize may be submitted to the Régie des loteries et courses du Quebec. All prizes will be awarded; winners will be notified by mail. No substitution of prizes is permitted. Winner selection is under the supervision of D.L. Blair, Inc., an independent judging organization whose decisions are final. Chances of winning in any drawing are dependent upon the number of eligible entries received. All prizes are valued in U.S. currency.

3. Potential winners must sign and return an Affidavit of Eligibility within 30 days of notification. In the event of non-compliance within this time period, the prize may be awarded to an alternate winner. Any prize or prize notification returned as undeliverable may result in the awarding of that prize to an alternate winner. By acceptance of their prize, winners consent to the use of their names, photographs or their likenesses for purposes of advertising, trade and promotion on behalf of Torstar Corp. without further compensation to the winner unless prohibited by law. Canadian winners must correctly answer a time-limited arithmetical question in order to be awarded a prize.

4. For a list of winners (available after 5/31/93), send a separate stamped, self-addressed envelope to: Barbary Wharf Sweepstakes Winners, P.O. Box 4526, Blair, NE 68009.

This month's special prize:
A Classic Wedgwood Tea Set!

Ever since Josiah Wedgwood first fired up his kilns in 1759, Wedgwood china has been the pride of England. Imagine how beautiful this set will look displayed in your home! It includes a tea pot, sugar bowl, creamer, and four cups and saucers, in Wedgwood's classic Royal Lapis pattern. This fine bone china tea set is a treasure you'll cherish always!

The Grand Prize:
An English Holiday for Two!

Visit London and tour the neighborhoods where the characters in *Barbary Wharf* work and fall in love. Visit the fabulous shops, the museums, the Tower of London and Buckingham Palace. . .enjoy theater and fine dining. And as part of your ten-day holiday, you'll be invited to lunch with the author, Charlotte Lamb! Round-trip airfare for two, first-class hotels, and meals are all included.

BARBARY WHARF
SWEEPSTAKES
OFFICIAL
ENTRY FORM

THIS MONTH'S SPECIAL PRIZE:

Classic Wedgwood Tea Set

NOTICE » Entry must be received by November 23, 1992.
Winner will be notified by December 1, 1992.

GRAND PRIZE:

A Vacation to England!

See prize descriptions on the back of this entry form.

Fill in your name and address below and return this
entry form with your invoice in the reply envelope provided.
Good luck!

NAME

ADDRESS

CITY   STATE/PROV.   ZIP/POSTAL CODE

(   )

DAYTIME PHONE NUMBER   (AREA CODE)

BW-M1